C000176703

Puffin Books
Editor: Kaye Webb

Flood Warning

Chomel, the school bully, was lying in bed waiting for his time fuse to explode outside M. Sala's door, when the first warning of the floods came. He didn't know that someone had spotted his trick, so just as the headmaster and his staff appeared in the dormitory to reassure their frightened pupils a 'shattering explosion lifted his mattress and deposited him on the floor gasping like a fish out of water.' The roar of laughter which followed almost drowned the gale which raged outside.

But that was the last chance anyone in the school had to laugh for a long time. Because soon the Loire burst its banks and the floods cut Château-Milon off from the world outside. Most of the school escaped to the woods, but a handful, including Chomel and M. Sala (the ineffectual little master whom nobody obeyed) were left behind in the old tower at the top of the school, with water rising outside the window, and no hope of rescue. Such circumstances can change characters, and so it was Hubert, the disdainful misfit, who appropriated a leaky boat and set out on the terrifying journey across vast blank miles of water in search of help.

As well as being an exciting story, this is a book about people and their hopes and weaknesses. For readers over ten, girls as well as boys.

Cover design by Charles Keeping

Translated from the French by
John Buchanan-Brown

Flood Warning

Paul Berna

Illustrated by Charles Keeping

Puffin Books
in association with The Bodley Head

Puffin Books, Penguin Books Ltd, Harmondsworth, Middlesex, England
Penguin Books Australia Ltd, Ringwood, Victoria, Australia
Penguin Books Canada Ltd, 41 Steelcase Road West, Markham, Ontario, Canada
Penguin Books (N.Z.) Ltd, 182–190 Wairau Road, Auckland 10, New Zealand

La Grande Alerte first published in France 1960
Published by The Bodley Head 1962
Published in Puffin Books 1966
Reprinted 1972, 1974, 1975

Made and printed in Great Britain by
C. Nicholls & Company Ltd
Set in Monotype Times

1 Monsieur Brossay, headmaster of Château-Milon, glanced at the clock out of the corner of his eye. Five past four. He opened his book, took a deep breath and slowly and deliberately went on with the lesson:

'Although the dangers, which in the past threatened our human ant-hill, have gradually grown less, thanks to the tide of progress, nonetheless this hard-won superiority is but a shield of straw. The history of the last hundred years shows us only too clearly that major natural disasters will always overwhelm mankind by their very unexpectedness or by their very scale, so quickly does each fresh generation forget or so shortsighted is it.'

This dramatic warning failed to impress his audience, the members of the Sixth.

Burly Muret was scribbling busily in his notebook, but what he wrote had little to do with Talhouët-Berger's *Human Geography*. All through the lesson he had been arranging and rearranging the school football team, his team. But in vain. Their fixture with the Cunault Football Club was upon them and still they were without a really good inside-right. It was a mess. Léo Lalande was the obvious

choice, but if he were brought into the forward line it would wreck the halves, and to repair the damage meant a whole series of moves which ended in the terrifying result that they would have an eleven in which no one, not even the goalie, was in his usual place. Muret could see only one way out and that was to plug the gap by bringing in his young brother, who played a brilliant game of inside-right in the Second XI. But unfortunately, good as he was, he had not got the physique to face ninety minutes of the wild-bull tackling of the beefy young farmers' sons from Cunault.

Lalande shared his desk to the left. He glanced at his captain's scribbles.

'What about Monsieur Boris?' he whispered suddenly.

This was the Languages master at Château-Milon, a brilliant sportsman and distinguished member of the Parisian 'Wanderers' club. Muret shrugged.

'No good,' he hissed. 'Boris is off to Paris this evening...'

Behind them sat the dreamer, Vignoles. His face was turned towards the tall windows which overlooked the courtyard. Eagerly he stared into the sunset which closed a lovely December day. The sky was a flat, hard gold lid pressed tight on the uplands of Anjou. A St Martin's summer had given ten days of almost spring-like warmth and brought Madame Brossay's ramblers out in flower. Between the yellow waves of empty orchard, the red of vine and peach still flamed along the slopes above Sermaize and Beaufort. The lofty plane trees in the courtyard had scarcely begun to shed their leaves. Through the leafy tracery Vignoles could see the road running to La Bohalle, the pink and grey roofs huddled below the massive bell-tower of La Ménitré, and in the distance, a mile or two beyond, the Loire, behind the rampart of its embankment. Every so often a tiny car would race along this skyline road from Saumur to Angers, to disappear behind the dark shoulder of the Arcy woods.

Five years before, Vignoles had come to Château-Milon on just such an evening. He had never left. His father had deposited him like a suitcase in a left-luggage office and had vanished into the whirl of business which took him from one corner of the globe to another. Every quarter brought a letter and a cheque. The kindness of the Brossays and the friendship of his schoolfellows had never made up for this lengthy exile. Now he was wondering yet again how to escape from Château-Milon.

The elegant Vicomte Hubert Boisson de Chazelles was asking himself the same question, if from very different motives. With his beaky nose and hair slicked back over his scalp, he had the air of a proud bird of prey as, knees carelessly crossed, legs stretched out beside his desk, thumb stuck between the buttons of his scarlet waistcoat, he listened to Monsieur Brossay and catalogued in his own mind the reasons for expulsion which had served him in the past. In five years Hubert had travelled far: three day-, six boarding-schools, and two crammers. Château-Milon would make the round dozen. His older cousin, Omer de Courson, had the week's use of his father's car and was due to kidnap him that evening when the day-boys went home. Would that be enough to exhaust even Monsieur Brossay's patience?

Just behind him Guillon and Montaigu, a picture of studious virtue, were peacefully engaged in conversation by means of a page of scribbling-paper which passed with question and answer from one to the other. Guillon had opened proceedings with six words which headlined the main news of the day.

'Rabbits' Eggs has got the sack!'

'Rot!' Montaigu scrawled in reply. 'We heard that a fortnight ago, but he's still here.'

'The juniors raised a monster riot in afternoon school. Old Brossay had to come over himself to calm things down.'

'It's happened before.'

'Yes, but it went too far this time. Rabbits' Eggs was in tears. Charlot Dubourg heard Monsieur Lacour tell Father Fabien, "Poor old Sala's going on Sunday".'

'Who started it?'

'Who do you think? That lout Chomel. He's a regular menace. I can't think why the juniors haven't taken him down a peg yet, and sided with Rabbits' Eggs. He can't help the way he looks and he isn't such a bad sort.'

'How did it start?'

'Chomel and Sardine shut Madame Juillet's two cats in the master's desk. They were all just waiting to watch Rabbits' Eggs lift the lid. Nothing happened for a quarter of an hour, the cats must have been asleep. Then one of them began to mew. Rabbits' Eggs went white as a sheet, opened the desk, the two cats popped out like jacks-in-the-box, the master screamed and fell off his chair, the classroom was in a shambles with twenty-five kids rolling in the aisles. You can picture it!'

'Gosh!' wrote Montaigu. 'Some picture!'

Guillon nudged him and nodded to the window.

Rabbits' Eggs and Father Fabien, the school Chaplain and Philosophy master, were pacing slowly up and down under the plane trees in the courtyard. With lowered head the little master listened as the ex-missionary preached away, his broad white beard wagging. Monsieur Sala had come with his degree, fresh from a provincial university, to find himself in charge of the prep-room and dormitory of Le Plessis, the junior house. It was a position through which many predecessors had passed, unable to stand for long the fire of the young toughs of Château-Milon. The odious Chomel had immediately nicknamed him Rabbits' Eggs. Monsieur Sala was neither particularly ugly, nor particularly good-looking, he had a kind heart and a keen brain, but all his good qualities were clouded by a shyness which he could not shake off and which made all he said and all he did look silly. The stupidest and most unfair nicknames can sometimes poison those to whom they are given. So everyone, even some of the masters, called him 'Rabbits' Eggs', and in the end poor Monsieur Sala had begun to live up to the stupidity of the nickname.

At the back of the class Charpenne studiously and carefully sketched the honest face of Monsieur Brossay. Vengeance guided his pencil. The headmaster had a lovely daughter, Edith, whose appearance on alternate Sundays fluttered the hearts of his fifty pupils. Charpenne was the only one to declare his love in a fortnightly sonnet which, for the price of a bar of milk chocolate, he had persuaded little Jozas to carry to his lady love. The baby of the Third had much freer access than anyone else to the headmaster's house and he would pass on the poems of de Musset or Ronsard that Charpenne had altered and signed in his own name. The first time this occurred Mademoiselle Edith had given the messenger another bar of chocolate and instructed him to pass on the sonnet to the cook, Madame Juillet, a powerful, rosy-cheeked female with a budding moustache and the same Christian name – Edith. All his other notes had taken the same route. Jozas had a corner in chocolate, while Charpenne was unaware that he had tuned his lyre for the kitchens alone. The surprisingly obstinate silence of his love he laid unjustly at the door of parental strictness and did not notice the peculiar looks which Madame Juillet had been giving him for some time.

He added a pimple to Monsieur Brossay's nose and sat back to admire his work before finishing off the drawing. Was he to turn the hard-hearted father into a jackal, a hyena, a hippo or a gorilla? Paper was scarce, so the artist decided in favour of a centipede's body armed with a pair of claws. This done, he slid the finished portrait under his left arm so that his neighbour could appreciate it.

Stolid, unexcitable Picard glanced at the masterpiece with a fishy eye and merely added a saucepan to the centipede's tail. His main concern at the moment was dietary. Would there, or would there not, be 'cannon-balls' for supper tonight? Madame Juillet fried these enormous rissoles of minced beef and mashed potato to perfection and such solid fare was Picard's favourite. It was one of the few things that could still the pangs of hunger which perpetually tormented his massive frame. 'Cannon-balls' had not been on the menu for a long time. Yes, perhaps tonight...

Monsieur Brossay finished what he had to say.

'Well, and how much of all that has sunk in?' he exclaimed, slapping his hand against the book. 'To my mind it should have made you think ...'

No one answered. He let his hands flop in a gesture of discouragement.

'Nothing,' he said angrily, 'nothing you've been taught in the last ten days seems to have been able to rouse the slightest spark. Now, what I've just been telling you could give any of you who showed an average keenness a very good essay subject. I'll speak to Father Fabien afterwards... For goodness' sake, wake up!'

The eight boys stared dully back at him without a flicker of interest. All they were waiting for was the bell for break.

Vignoles still stared at the sky in a preoccupied fashion. Monsieur Brossay was right. The last ten days had been too warm and fine. At Château-Milon, in common with everywhere else, all they had wanted to do was to watch the golden hours of the dying year slip past. There was hardly a chill in the night air even when the mist gathered in ragged patches along the banks of the River Authion. The wind itself was dead.

Vignoles half turned his head to watch the sunset. In spite of himself he had grown to love the land of his exile, and none knew better than he the subtle signs which heralded the changing seasons. This evening there was not a cloud and yet the brassy sky foreboded something. Vignoles had never felt the atmosphere hang so heavy on the broad plains of Anjou.

In the classroom next door the Mathematics master, Monsieur Lacour, scrawled furious equations on the blackboard, oblivious of background noises. The Upper Fifth could not take its eyes off one of their number. It was Jeantet's turn to ring the bell and the others threateningly pointed alternately to the clock and to the door.

As soon as the quarter-hour came up Jeantet seized his books and was out of the door like lightning. He sprinted across the courtyard to where Mérovée's Tower stood at the gateway and tugged the rope attached to Cunégonde, the bell whose silvery peal split the working day into its eight periods. The bell-ringing was one of the rituals of Château-Milon and for the seniors, who took this duty in turns, a keenly coveted privilege. The first time the mighty Picard performed it he had brought Cunégonde crashing down thirty feet into a geranium bed, in which she buried herself like a heavy-calibre shell. From then on he was relieved of this duty. Cunégonde's strokes were always welcome, but that peaceful Saturday night there was a special note to her peal which several of the more imaginative boys were to remember.

Château-Milon's five classrooms emptied on the first notes and a horde of juniors from the Third and Lower Fourth poured across the courtyard to storm the Hall, where Madame Juillet and her daughter Pauline were serving tea.

A squad of day-boys, a dozen in all, headed for the cars parked outside the gate on the narrow road to La Bohalle. Cunningly Hubert Boisson de Chazelles mingled with them, his eyes anxiously searching for his cousin Omer's big blue saloon. There was no sign of it, nor could the escaper pick him out among the parents gathered at the railings. He turned on his heel, cursing Omer and all his works. Another long and killingly dull week in this dung-heap!

Old Monsieur Corzon, the school bursar, with Monsieur Lacour, Monsieur Boris and Monsieur Simon made their way in pairs towards the headmaster's house, where the masters' tea was waiting. Father Fabien and Monsieur Sala brought up the rear, the latter still as miserable as ever. Madame Brossay had just brought Edith back from Nantes, and the windows of her drawing-room shone bright in the gathering dusk.

Muret and his friend Lalande caught Monsieur Boris at the doorway.

'Can't find a right-half!' Lalande announced gloomily. 'Those clodhoppers from Cunault will give us the beating of our lives tomorrow.'

'That won't do you any harm,' Monsieur Boris said, laughing. 'Nothing like an occasional licking!'

'Be decent,' Muret begged him. 'Just one more game for us . . .'

'You'll be going to Paris next Sunday anyway,' Lalande added.

Monsieur Boris turned to the other master as if to call on him to witness his lack of will-power. Then he half noticed the peculiar glow of the distant sunset.

'All right,' he said resignedly. 'I'll turn out at right-half for you and we'll try to beat these young heavyweights, since you seem so scared of them. I expect we'll have another fine day tomorrow, so don't let's waste it!'

Muret and Lalande thanked him effusively and made off at top speed. The football team had just rounded the corner of the building, passing the old ball they used for practice from one to the other. The school football pitch lay beyond the gardens on a worn strip of meadowland bounded by the bushy banks of the Authion. The evening break was too short for a proper game, so all the captain could do was set two lines of attackers against picked defenders at either end. His enthusiasts were soon after the ball, oblivious of the dusk which gradually invaded the pitch.

The others spent the three-quarters of an hour as their fancy dictated. There was basket-ball, or the whole courtyard through which to run shrieking, while the aged plane trees gazed down on the old château and its new buildings and games fields. Mérovée's Tower, a creeper-covered mill of local stone, had been saved by Monsieur Brossay to add a tone of feudal antiquity to his property. It was a noble ruin, although its wooden beams were so rotten that it was placed out of bounds to the boys.

Guillon and Montaigu were chatting to Charlot Dubourg outside the dining-hall. It was not long before they had agreed to take a strong hand in the row about Monsieur Sala.

'Come here!' Charlot called to his young brother, Kiki, prime mover of any mischief among the juniors.

Reluctantly Kiki came up, his mouth full of bun and chocolate.

'You've done a fine thing, I must say!' Guillon growled and twisted his ear. 'For the whole term you've been ragging poor old Rabbits' Eggs. You've no excuse. He's a decent bloke. Nobody minds the odd rag. You let off steam and even the toughest masters see the joke. But you went a darn sight too far. Monsieur Brossay's given Sala the sack – all because of you. Is that what you want? The poor little man needs to earn a living like anyone else and now *you've* done him out of a job!'

Kiki Dubourg hung his head.

'Nothing to do with me.' He was rather ashamed. 'Chomel and his gang pinched Ma Juillet's cats. Me and the others just sat back and watched the fun...'

'Well,' his brother cut in coldly, 'tell them the news. I expect they'll be delighted. And tell them to watch out. Rabbits' Eggs is going to take his last prep this evening. If you rag him again you won't have Monsieur Brossay on your tracks, you'll have the Sixth. Oh, and tell Chomel we're going to give him the biggest hiding of his life tomorrow night... Get!'

On the edge of the courtyard sniggering groups discussed the joke they had played on Monsieur Sala. Kiki made his round from one to the other, muttering mysteriously. The decree of the Sixth took the wind out of the sails of even the cheekiest. Meanwhile the sky had changed colour and a blood-red sunset tinged the buildings like a stage set.

The solitary Vignoles walked slowly towards Mérovée's Tower. The last of the day-boys had departed. The double iron gates, set midway between the old mill and the chapel, were being shut by Monsieur Juillet. The cook's husband was a good-natured mountain of a man with a walrus moustache. Caretaker, chauffeur, head gardener and odd-job man at Château-Milon, he was fond of the lonely boy who spent all his holidays at school so uncomplainingly and without sinking into lazy boredom. The pair paused and gazed through the railings at the uplands glowing in the sunset. Evening brought heavier traffic to the far-off road along the embankment.

'Funny weather!' Vignoles murmured and sniffed the air. 'Another week of this and we'll have all the flowers out again.'

'Don't count on it!' grunted Monsieur Juillet. 'This weather's not natural. Haven't you noticed? You can smell a storm in the air.'

'Oh, no! We'll have another fine Sunday . . .'

'Yes – for the ducks! I just heard the latest weather forecast. Midday today it was raining in Biarritz. It'll be a damp day when you wake up tomorrow.'

'That'll spoil the game,' said Vignoles. 'I'm hopeless if the ground's heavy.'

'It won't be just a drizzle either, you mark my words,' Monsieur Juillet chuckled.

Picard, hungry as ever, walked round the corner of the building to the kitchens. He wanted reassurance. Job and Yvon, the Trévidic brothers, were returning from the garden with a great crate of lettuce for salad. They had started life as farm labourers, but had been promoted at Château-Milon to kitchen-portering and waiting in the dining-hall. Hence they knew what the menu would be twenty-four hours in advance. But Picard did not dare expose his greed by questioning them. Instead he followed them with an innocent air as far as the kitchen. The door opened upon a glutton's paradise. Flour-coated 'cannon-balls' were marshalled in long lines down two tables, at one of which Madame Juillet was vigorously shaping the last of them. She saw his delighted face as he peered round the door-post.

'You're in luck!' she winked. 'Two each. That should set you up....'

Charpenne scanned the courtyard for his messenger. He had composed a 'Fifth Sonnet for Edith'. The last two verses were of his own making, the rest had been lifted wholesale from Lamartine. As though by accident little Jozas crossed his path and at once the note changed hands.

'I'll have to put up my price.' His baby face was grave. 'It's much more risky at tea-time. It'll cost you two bars of chocolate.'

But the lover did not bargain and Jozas sped off, mounting the steps to the front door two at a time. At that instant Charpenne pulled out his handkerchief, and with it another note. As he unfolded it he felt his hair stand on end in horror. He had muddled his pockets and the sonnet was still there. His beloved Edith was going to get a centipede-bodied portrait of her worthy father.

'Come back!' Charpenne shouted and plunged after Jozas.

But it was too late. The messenger had vanished through the glass door.

Five minutes later the portrait had gone the rounds of the drawing-room, for Father Fabien's curiosity had been too strong for Edith. The masters were highly amused and Monsieur Brossay had the good sense to laugh loudest of them all.

'I recognize Charpenne's hand,' he said sarcastically, 'but who added the saucepan? Ugh! Father Fabien, be honest, do I really look like a centipede?'

The onlookers laughed, and unscrewing his fountain pen, he added to the head of the sketch: *My congratulations to the artist*. And then at the foot he wrote: *Take 8 hours' detention* and signed his name. Monsieur Simon was due to take senior prep that night, so he handed it to him saying, 'Be kind enough to return this to Charpenne. Perhaps next time he'll aim his shafts elsewhere.'

Charpenne, huddled below the open drawing-room windows, could not but realize that all his schemes had gone awry.

Nightfall brought no drop in the temperature. The stifling air weighed more and more heavily upon the boys in the courtyard. Madame Juillet's two cats stalked edgily round the flower beds, eyes flashing, spitting if anyone came near them.

The light grew less and less, but still the footballers battled on. At last Muret had to call a halt a quarter of an hour early. Night had closed in suddenly and they could not even see the ball. As they walked back they were in high spirits about the outcome of the match next day.

'We've got them cold!' Gontier, the First XI goalie, announced. 'The dry ground'll let us show a bit of class and with Boris in the half-back line we could give away three goals and still lick Cunault!'

'If it's going to be as hot as it was today watch your wind!' called the right-back, Raynard, as he slipped on his sweater. 'Last Sunday we were all on our knees by the second half.'

Monsieur Sala sipped his tea shyly in a corner of the Brossays' drawing-room. Already he no longer felt part of the school, where, had things fallen out otherwise, life might have been both pleasant and easy. He deposited his cup and removed his glasses to rub his tired eyes. Once he had got rid of the thick lenses which gave him such a stupidly heavy look, his face relaxed and he seemed a different person altogether.

'You should take them off more often in front of the young ruffians in your house,' Edith murmured. 'With those great windscreens no one can see how nice you are.'

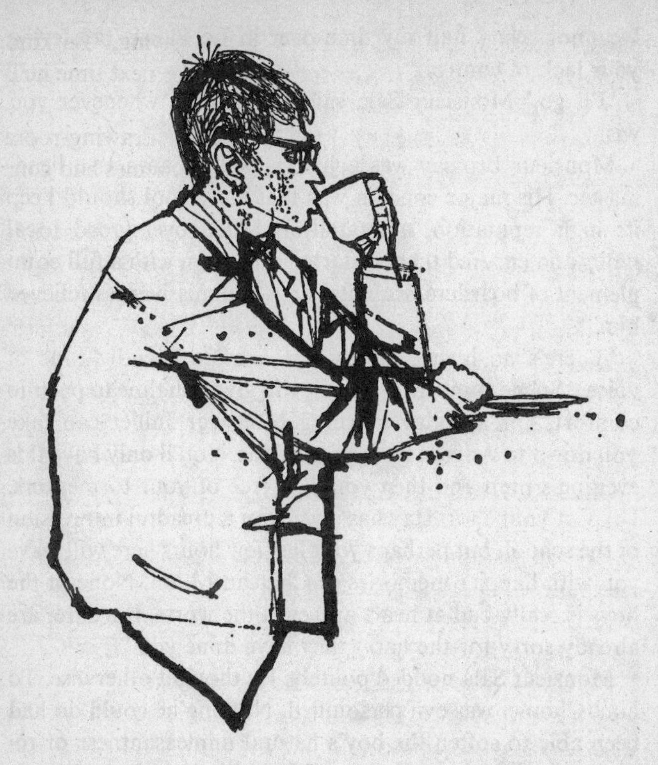

'It's a bit late in the day, now,' sighed the little man.

Monsieur Brossay signalled to him above the heads of the others. Monsieur Sala circled the drawing-room unnoticed and rejoined him in the headmaster's study. The latter seemed upset.

'I really am most distressed,' he said, not looking at Monsieur Sala, 'but you must agree that this situation cannot continue. I gave you a fortnight to bring the ringleaders to book. The reprieve has been useless. Your house is a permanent source of disorder. This is not entirely your fault and I shall see that the guilty are punished as they deserve. But

I cannot spend half my time over in Le Plessis bolstering your lack of control.'

'I'll go,' Monsieur Sala said resignedly, 'whenever you wish...'

Monsieur Brossay was a just as well as an active headmaster. His major concern was that his school should keep its high reputation, a reputation which overspread local limits and ensured that he started each term with a full complement of boarders. Rabbits' Eggs' submissiveness relieved him.

'There's no hurry,' he said in a more friendly tone of voice. 'Spend tomorrow here: it will give you time to pack in comfort. On Monday morning Monsieur Juillet can take you down to Angers station in the car. You'll only have this evening's prep and then you'll be free of your tormentors. I expect your short stay has given you a dreadful impression of the school, but perhaps your last few hours here will leave you with happier memories of Château-Milon. None of the boys is really bad at heart and even the worst, I'm sure, are already sorry for the harm they have done you.'

Monsieur Sala nodded politely. He thought otherwise. To him, Chomel was evil personified. Nothing he could do had been able to soften the boy's natural unpleasantness or remove his ridiculous grudge against the timid little schoolmaster imprisoned in his own shyness.

When the two men re-entered the drawing-room they had changed the subject. They found that Madame Brossay had turned on more lights to cheer the party. For, although the same friendly group was gathered that evening as had forgathered every other evening that term, most of them felt an uneasiness as of some strange presence in the room. Father Fabien's deep laugh sounded a little forced. Edith hardly responded to the teasing of the masters. Monsieur Boris to his amazement found himself looking over his shoulder to see who had brushed past him when there was nobody there. For an instant Madame Brossay glanced round to see if there was an uninvited guest. Through the open windows they could hear the boys playing in the courtyard, but even their voices rang flat and showed that their games were half-hearted.

'This warm weather is really most unseasonable,' old Monsieur Corzon complained, and dabbed a damp forehead with his handkerchief.

'Did you see?' said Madame Brossay. 'I've two new buds on the rambler on the south wall of the chapel. The sunshine should bring them out tomorrow.'

Monsieur Brossay wriggled his wrist to see the time and as the minutes ticked away Monsieur Sala felt the muscles of his stomach tighten as they always did at the prospect of taking prep.

Outside Jeantet strode towards Mérovée's Tower through a horde of clutching juniors who shouted to him to add an extra minute or two to the break. Cunégonde rang out, but with a muffled note that seemed to come from a long way off.

Vignoles heard it from where he stood motionless outside La Vallière, the senior house. His ears were pricked, his every sense alert. The peal of the bell underlined the vague feeling of disquiet which had been growing in him hour by hour that evening. 'Something is going to happen,' he thought.

At the last stroke of the bell, night fell like a curtain on Château-Milon.

Monsieur Sala was among the last to leave the Brossays' drawing-room. His companions, Lacour and Simon, shrugged pityingly as they watched the condemned man walk slowly over to Le Plessis.

There was a deathly hush in the prep-room. Twenty-five heads bent over twenty-five desks never so much as moved when the door closed gently. At times Rabbits' Eggs would dearly have loved to take his revenge by caning each one individually and reminding them between strokes of the outrages they had inflicted upon him. 'What devilry are they plotting now?' he wondered as he stepped up to his desk.

He distrusted calm, which generally preceded a storm of ragging, but Chomel's spotty face and bullet head were half hidden behind an atlas and the little man sighed with relief as he sat down. Out came the weighty volumes which seldom left him. Behind his undistinguished exterior lurked a modest but brilliant intellect. Monsieur Sala was secretly writing a philosophical treatise on 'Modern survivals of Kantian thought'. The very dryness of his theme helped him to forget the practical jokes which were his daily fare.

The first hour passed peacefully. The hush which opened it had given way to a dull mutter, not of open revolt but of the hundred and one slight sounds of a busy classroom, twenty-five bodies shuffling in their desks, feet scraping, yawns, books or pens falling, whispered requests, the squeak of a desk as someone used a rubber hard. Still all that could be seen of Chomel was his snub nose.

Monsieur Sala gathered hope. Only one more hour and he would escape this hell on earth. He sank back once more into *The Critique of Pure Reason* and in the end forgot a world in which he could do nothing right. To an unprejudiced observer who discounted the difference in years, there was no difference between him and the twenty-five other hard-working pupils. And that was how someone must have seen him.

The first eruption caught him on this footing and in some strange way put him back in his own schooldays.

'Sala!' a voice trumpeted from the end of the room. 'Take a hundred lines!'

A gale of laughter greeted this sally. Rabbits' Eggs lost his place in his book and looked up open-mouthed. The whole room tossed before his shortsighted eyes like a stormy sea. Had he left his desk he would have been finished, so he sat still. Skinny, pallid Chomel stood on his desk to conduct a farewell performance in which good and bad elements were alike united. Despairingly Monsieur Sala raised an arm to gesture them to silence, but his mute appeal only made them redouble the din. He saw that he was doomed to the shame of running off to the main building to implore Monsieur Brossay's aid.

When the noise was at its height unlooked-for help arrived from outside. A rumble rose in gusts above the cat-calls. Something was happening in the courtyard, something most unusual. The hoots grew fewer and fewer. Chomel sat down. The ringleader of the ragging was the biggest coward in Château-Milon. The boys looked around at one another in scared astonishment. For a moment Monsieur Sala thought he had tamed his tormentors, but having closed his books he could see from their strained expressions that this was not the case. He looked through the window, but could see nothing, for there was nothing to see.

An instant later all was changed. A howling blast struck the vicinity and rattled the window-panes. Almost at once an insecurely fastened window crashed open and slammed against the wall, and a gale of wind swept the desks. Then all was silent once more. A few of the braver boys approached the gaping window curiously. There was only the night beyond it. Behind the château, over the gardens, the sounds disappeared in a dull rumble like a distant charge of cavalry.

Incisively Monsieur Sala rose from his desk. He could not explain it, but the wildness of the night had sparked in him,

for the first time in his life, a terrible courage. He banged the window shut and turned to the astonished boys.

'Back to work all of you! Anyone who moves or makes a sound will be in trouble!'

His voice cut the silence in accents so chillingly different that it seemed to come from another person. Thereupon he boldly strode down the aisle between the desks to hasten those who were taking an unduly long time to pick up their scattered books. Chomel happened to be in his path and thought it clever not to move. A lout of sixteen, who had already failed his remove two years running, he was a good head taller than the master. Monsieur Sala seized one of his ears and slowly pulled him to his feet. Nobody could tell where he got his inspiration from, but at last he had his revenge.

'Monsieur Chomel,' he said carefully, enunciating each word, 'you are very big, and very nasty, and your nastiness seems to have attracted the worst elements in the form. But there is many a slip between cup and lip, and so do not be too sure that I shall leave this school before you do.'

Chomel sat down hastily and did not stir again.

2 In La Vallière the seniors were working peacefully when the night erupted around Château-Milon. The eight lights in the courtyard were only put on when the covered way between houses, classrooms and dining-hall was in use, so that all was inky darkness outside. In his anxiety to know what had happened Monsieur Simon became a little flustered.

'Sit still, I'm going to see what it was...'

But the group of seniors took no notice of what he said and followed him quietly. Slowly they went downstairs, came out of the door and peered cautiously about them. All was still. The atmosphere was as oppressive as ever. From the gardens came a twitter of birds, but there was not another sound. The sky was a mass of stars to the distant horizon. Vignoles looked up. The last dead leaves were raining down from the tall plane trees, revolving slowly like a swarm of butterflies as they were caught in the light which streamed in bars of gold from the windows. At that moment Father Fabien came out of chapel carrying his breviary.

'Did you hear it?' Monsieur Simon asked him.

'It was only a puff of wind,' the ex-missionary chuckled.

'That's what I thought, but you don't get a puff of wind as strong as that all on its own. Yet it's dead calm now.'

'Let's wait,' said Vignoles. 'The second may come any minute now.'

'An earthquake?' Lalande suggested.

'You'd have felt that a bit differently,' growled Father Fabien. 'I *know* what I'm talking about!'

'Perhaps it was an explosives factory going up somewhere,' Guillon put in. 'Remember the explosion last year in the Marne.'

'It could be,' said Monsieur Simon. 'But the nearest factory is fifty or sixty miles away, near Châtellerault.'

'Blast has a funny way of travelling,' Montaigu piped up in the background. 'We ought to switch on the news. They're bound to say if something serious has happened.'

In the distance Monsieur Brossay and Monsieur Corzon came out of the headmaster's house. They were deep in conversation as they turned to peer anxiously into the night. They did not notice the group on the other side of the courtyard, and a few moments later they went indoors.

'Upstairs!' Monsieur Simon ordered.

They went with deliberate slowness, laughing at the sudden scare which had rippled the life of the school. Charpenne, who had been given his centipede – and his eight hours' detention – prayed with all his heart for some minor act of God to enliven the gloomy Sunday which fate seemed to hold in store for him.

Picard snuffed the air like a hound. Behind the building the 'cannon-balls' were in the pan, and a delicious smell of frying made his mouth water.

'It'll be a lovely day for beating Cunault,' Muret said and pointed to the clear sky.

'And plenty of spectators,' Lalande added with ill-concealed delight.

'No,' Vignoles muttered under his breath.

The sudden gust had only deepened his misgivings. Somewhere in the countryside around a threat was gathering and the boy realized that it might materialize at any moment in some terrifying form or another. The approach of danger did not make him nervous, however; rather he felt a burning desire to know just what this peril which chance was about to hurl upon them could be.

At seven o'clock the joyous strokes of Cunégonde announced supper. Jeantet had no sooner done with the bell-rope than he pulled a switch and the buildings sprang into light around a courtyard carpeted in yellow. As the boys came tumbling out of their prep-rooms they eyed the transformation with delight – the blast of wind an hour before had stripped the plane trees, and their branches gleamed bare against the starry sky.

'That's me for the sweeping-party,' Charpenne sighed. 'Monsieur Brossay's bound to give me the job of clearing the courtyard... What a Sunday!'

The two Trévidic brothers could be seen in long white aprons behind the uncurtained windows of the dining-hall. Job opened the double doors and began frenziedly to tinkle his bell.

'Hurry up and sit down!' called Monsieur Simon, and clapped his hands to summon the sluggards.

Never was a meal more lively or more noisy. At every table, including the masters', the events of the evening were hotly argued between optimists and pessimists.

'I'd just gone out,' Yvon Trévidic told the Sixth, 'to the end of the kitchen garden with a bucket of waste. Without a word of a lie the wind blew it right out of my hands and nearly took me with it!'

His hands were still shaking.

'What happened next?' Guillon asked in astonishment.

'Next? Nothing! I hadn't time to think what had happened when it was all over. It was no joke, I can tell you.'

Pauline, the Juillets' gawky, grown-up daughter, waited on the masters.

'There wasn't anything on the radio,' she told them. 'I didn't leave the kitchen till the news was over...'

'I can't believe it!' Monsieur Simon burst out, staring round at the others. 'What about the weather forecast?'

'Not too good. Downpour in the south-west.'

Monsieur Sala kept his nose to his plate and himself to himself. It had always been difficult to get a sensible word out of the timid little man, when the most everyday questions put him out of countenance. In the end the others had come to respect his self-enforced isolation. The news of his dismissal had gone round, but no one as yet dared express a sympathy which would in any case have appeared a trifle forced.

The arrival of the 'cannon-balls' put an end to all argument. There was a hum of anticipation. The Sixth Form table was ready. Each was waiting to put Picard to the test. Such solid fare was a little too much for the fastidious Hubert Boisson de Chazelles and he started things off.

'No, really, I'm not hungry. Would anyone like my helping? Don't be shy...'

Then began an exchange of rather too obvious politeness. Even the hungriest declined this second helping, but only after such hesitation as made the glutton tremble for fear they would accept. In the end the two scorned 'cannon-balls' came to rest on Picard's plate and he fell upon them without a side-glance. Montaigu only ate one of his and sent the other round the table. It followed the same route. Lalande did the same; a little later Guillon copied him, as did Vignoles and Muret. The whole business of the centipede had so taken away his appetite that Charpenne left his 'cannon-balls' to grow cold. By now Picard was sadly picking at the fragments on his plate. Suddenly he caught sight of two more miraculous and generous offerings and swooped on them like a vulture on a pair of new-born lambs.

'Take it easy!' said Loulou Muret, refilling the glutton's glass. 'Have a drop of cider to thin the mixture. It's giving us stomach-ache to watch you putting it away.'

Picard, quite undismayed, merely nodded as his jaws went champing on. He cleared his plate in fine style and then was rather annoyed to see that all around him the others were also empty. Job came past with their bowls of salad.

'You haven't any spuds left?' the prodigy asked and stopped Job in his tracks.

But the neighbouring table rallied round, and Dubourg

senior passed him a plate holding five more 'cannon-balls'.

'Stop!' groaned Montaigu, burying his head in his hands. 'You'll have a stroke.'

But Picard took not a scrap of notice and tackled them at the same deliberate pace. When he had finished Muret called to him in delighted surprise:

'Sixteen "cannon-balls"! You've beaten last month's record! To see you, old chap, anyone would think you hadn't had food for a week.'

'I just have to eat a lot,' Picard explained, unaffected by his feat. 'I can't help it. And some meals are about as much good to me as a cup of hot air. So I stoke up when I can...'

'Well tonight's dinner should keep you going for a good long time!' Vignoles concluded and they all laughed.

Chomel sat among the juniors, pale and tense. He picked at his food and glared disdainfully at his neighbours whom he blamed for the failure of the rag.

'I've still got a couple of thunder-flashes left,' he whispered to his crony, Sardy, or Sardine, the clown of the class. 'We'll keep them for tonight. Rabbits' Eggs never turns his light out before midnight, so all you've got to do is lay them against his door. I'll set them off at the right moment. I shan't have to move an inch. Twenty-four foot of fuse'll take a good twenty minutes to burn, so we'll have all that time to wake these cowardly rats up and get them ready for the big bang.'

'Right!' said Sardine.

There was half an hour's break between the end of supper and bedtime. Monsieur Brossay trusted his Sixth Formers, who were free to stretch their legs in the garden or to use the billiard-room in his own house if they did not make too much noise. The others went out into the courtyard or back to the day-rooms of their respective houses, where there was a master to keep an eye on them until they went to bed. That evening Monsieur Boris suggested, unprompted, that he lend Monsieur Sala a hand during the interval. Together they rounded up their flock and shepherded it indoors.

'You know I'm going on Monday?' said Monsieur Sala.

The other nodded.

'We're all really very sorry about it, believe me. Two months isn't long enough to get to know someone properly, but I'm sure a lot of us are going to miss you.'

'Those won't!' Monsieur Sala grunted, nodding towards the juniors tumbling through the door.

'Don't be too sure,' said Monsieur Boris. 'It's so hard to know what's going on in their heads. I agree you sometimes only need one boy to poison a whole form. But however bad his influence, he can be brought round, you know, to get rid of it as if it were a cold.'

'In Chomel's case it's bubonic plague!'

'He needs a severe shock to change him. And he'll get it sooner or later. Often it's only something very slight...'

'Someone else will benefit from his reformation,' the little man sighed resignedly.

'What do you plan to do?'

'I'm going back to my parents' in Savoy. A fortnight's rest will put me right. Then I'll try to get a coaching job in Grenoble or somewhere. Just something to keep the wolf from the door.'

'Some very good friends of mine are on the University staff at Grenoble,' said Monsieur Boris. 'I'll write to them. They're bound to be able to put you on to something.'

The dormitory of Le Plessis held three lines of ten beds, each divided from the other by shoulder-level partitions in pitch-pine. Monsieur Sala's room was on the landing and opened immediately on to the dormitory through a sliding door with a long white curtain in front of it, thus enabling him to keep an eye upon possible unrest and to head off sham sleep-walkers at any time of night.

He stood in the doorway of his room and watched from a distance the bustle of boys at wash-basins. There seemed to be nothing afoot. Chomel dabbed his face, towelled himself vigorously, and retired to his bed, the end one on the right. Good riddance, thought Monsieur Sala.

He was able to turn the lights out at nine o'clock, leaving only the night-light to diffuse its bluish glimmer. All seemed quiet and the first snores filled the four corners of the dormitory. He left only a crack of the sliding door open and pulled the curtain right across. His bedside light hardly shone through the curtained gap which divided him from the slumbering boys. Buried in his massive tomes, his card index open, his notes spread out, he was unaware of a slight rustle outside his door. At ten o'clock the barefooted Sardine had tiptoed close to him, had placed the thunder-flashes with infinite stealth against the door and then backed away, unrolling the fuse until it reached Chomel's bedside.

'Wait till he switches out his light. I won't do anything

before then,' the latter hissed diabolically. 'You can cut my arms off if this doesn't bring down the ceiling!'

Then all was peace once more.

If Sardine had conducted his operations in silence, Kiki Dubourg and little Jozas went to work even more quietly, and their activities were much more prolonged. The juniors had decided upon counter-measures to protect their housemaster, without foregoing the pleasure of the explosion, from which great things were expected. In short, fifteen minutes later the fuse now went full circle, snaking from one cubicle to the next. Chomel still had one end, but no idea that the two thunder-flashes now nestled under his own bed, just below the sag of his posterior. Meantime he hugged himself at the thought of lighting the train as he lay snug in bed.

The first floor of the senior house, La Vallière, contained a smaller dormitory and a number of rooms with two or three beds in each, which were reserved for members of the Sixth. Vignoles had one of the lightest, with windows on the corner of the wing facing the doorway of Mérovée's Tower. He managed to share it happily with Charpenne and Boisson de Chazelles, despite the latter's fussiness, appalling affectation, and precocious snobbery.

All three had gone up to their room together after a short stroll in the gardens. The atmosphere was as oppressive as ever, but there was still not a cloud in the sky and the uncanny calm of the countryside held the promise of another lovely day.

Hubert was the first to undress somewhat wearily.

'Do you two really think it was a whirlwind or did we dream it up?' he asked as he slid between the sheets.

'I couldn't care less,' Charpenne grunted. 'Château-Milon's beginning to get me down. Here we are in the back of the beyond...'

'What does the old lag say?'

Vignoles shrugged. He had merely removed his coat and now leaned out of the window, his elbows on the sill, to enjoy the silence of the night. Charpenne hurriedly washed and then threw himself on top of his bed and lit a cigarette. Vignoles watched the lights go out one by one. Stealthily Madame Juillet's cats crossed the patch of light which still fell from the kitchen windows and cast their shadows in monstrous exaggeration on the wall of the dining-hall. The murmured conversation of a group of masters was lost in the darkness of the courtyard. Soon someone called to them from the front door and they scattered, their footsteps whispering in the thick carpet of dead leaves.

Vignoles went to bed in his turn. He switched off the light and then lay stretched in the darkness, unable to close his eyes to the square of sky that shimmered beyond the open window. A nagging anxiety kept him awake. All the same, at about eleven, his eyes began gradually to close. He must have slept for some five or six minutes when he awoke with a start, his face bathed in sweat. In that short time everything had changed. Startled, he sat up, staring at the black patch of window. The stars had vanished from the sky.

The night had grown darker still, and seemed to have closed in on them. The lofty plane trees stood in stony immobility, their silvery trunks barely marking the inky pit of the courtyard. But somewhere in the distant countryside there were stirrings and a ceaseless murmur as of a mighty army on the march.

Charpenne was awakened by the creak of a floorboard beside his bed.

'What are you up to?'

Vignoles tiptoed to the window.

'I think we're in for it!' he answered. 'Take a look at this...'

At that very instant, in Le Plessis, Monsieur Sala had switched out his light, slid the door open a crack, and twitched aside the curtain to make sure his unruly charges had settled down. Everyone was apparently fast asleep. Quietly he got into bed and soon was dead to the world. A moment later the dark line of the partitions was broken by two tousled heads.

'The coast's clear,' Sardine whispered.

A match cracked and flickered in the blue half-light and almost immediately went out. Chomel glanced at the luminous dial of his watch. Another twenty minutes and the mine would explode in the little master's ear, the juniors would be jumping out of bed screaming like fiends, Rabbits' Eggs would blunder panic-stricken through the curtains in his old-fashioned nightshirt, his rescuers with the best will in the world would flood his room, and it would all be bound to end up in one tremendous pillow-fight. Chomel snuggled down in a seventh heaven at the mere thought. The glowing tip of the fuse made its slow journey over the floorboards and soon vanished round the end of the partition. Things were running smoothly: all he had to do was wait...

Monsieur Sala was having a most peculiar dream. There, at the desks in his classroom, sat a score of farm animals, cows and calves, pigs, chickens and donkeys, all kicking up the most appalling din, egged on by an ugly bearded billy-goat, who looked exactly like Chomel. In a wild burst of rage Monsieur Sala leaped from his seat and, brandishing a horse-whip, began with superhuman energy to lay into the mob. The lash cracked as he drove back his enemies, who roared, brayed, or mooed their various protests. As he caught the billy-goat a blow on its long nose, the creature with one panther-like leap shot through the window, the panes falling in a shower of broken glass. The noise awoke Monsieur

Sala. He jumped out of bed, his heart pounding in alarm.

One of the tall dormitory windows had been blown in. The wild blast of wind set the curtain ballooning. Outside, the gale burst its bonds. Its first shock fell upon Château-Milon with a noise like thunder. Driven before it, a hail of flying débris battered the walls and roofs with a ceaseless rattle.

Monsieur Sala at once switched on the ceiling lights, thrust himself into his shabby dressing-gown, and emerged from his room. Inside the dormitory the wind howled with terrifying power through the wreckage and blew the curtains level with the ceiling. Some of the boys were sitting up in bed, fearful and bewildered. As he made his way to the shattered window to examine the extent of the damage, a gust blew him against the nearest partition. It belonged to Kiki Dubourg. The bedclothes were thick with glittering pieces of broken glass.

'Are you hurt?' he asked the boy. 'Quickly! Strip your bed and get away from here!'

Kiki was all right, he was only scared to death. Monsieur Sala shifted Jozas from the danger zone and another boy as well, and packed them off to the empty beds at the other end of the dormitory.

At first-floor level a huge branch had snapped off one of the plane trees and had come crashing full force against the unprotected window. This battering-ram stuck three feet inside the room, a mass of twigs and branches. The wind howled through the hole, blowing in a rain of dead leaves, bits of straw and other garden refuse and filling the room with a choking cloud of dust.

Monsieur Sala called Martin and Desbois, the two eldest and most sensible boys, over to him.

'Stand by the door while I'm away,' he told them, 'and see that *nobody* goes out. I'm going downstairs to get help.'

Meanwhile the lights went on again all round the courtyard, across which anxious voices called. Hurried footsteps clattered along the covered way. But all the bustle was drowned in the roar of the gale as it battered against the building, making it shake to its foundations. The gusts swirled round Mérovée's Tower and set Cunégonde swinging and mournfully ringing like the bell of a fogbound schooner.

As Monsieur Sala came down into the hall he was stopped by the sight of Monsieur Boris and Monsieur Lacour. The two men were half-dressed and struggled through the doorway almost on hands and knees, as the wind rushed in with them and threw them against one another. All three had to use every ounce of strength to shut the door again. It fought them like a frightened beast.

'Don't go out!' Monsieur Boris told Monsieur Sala. 'We nearly killed ourselves coming over. The air's a mass of wreckage. I saw half a ton of fencing whistle past my head!'

'One of the big windows in my dormitory's been smashed in,' announced Monsieur Sala. 'Unless we do something pretty soon the gale's going to wreck the whole of that floor.'

'Let's go and see.'

As they entered the dormitory they had the full force of the wind in their faces as it rushed unhindered through the broken casement. Almost at once there was a crack as a flying tile or piece of wood smashed a pane in the next window and above the thunder of the storm the wind rose to a high-pitched shriek. It whirled the clothes off the nearest beds in all directions, while a dozen frightened boys in pyjamas or shirt-tails huddled behind Martin and Desbois at the other end of the dormitory. Monsieur Sala at once made them lie down on the other empty beds. A few still slept the sleep of the just, their bedclothes around their ears, and they had to be woken up, since things might at any moment go from bad to worse.

Below them the hall door crashed open. Monsieur Brossay had arrived, and with him Monsieur Juillet and the Trévidic brothers.

'It took us six minutes to cover the fifty yards from my house to here,' he gasped. 'There's not a pane of glass left in the covered way...'

The headmaster's face was haggard, his scanty fair hair was ludicrously rumpled by the wind, and his appearance caused the boys and masters much secret amusement. He forced himself to appear outwardly calm and assured, and grinned encouragingly at the youngest. His orders were speedily carried out. Monsieur Juillet called for volunteers and went down to his workshop in the cellar. The wind beat against Job and Yvon as they set to at once to hack at the limb of the plane tree until it toppled into the courtyard.

The working-party soon reappeared with a dozen stout planks and plenty of three-inch nails. In a few minutes they had closed the gap as best they could and had strengthened each of the other windows with crosspieces. At last the dormitory regained the appearance of peace, despite the sinister sounds of the storm outside. Within, the wind hissing through the cracks made a noise like a steam-engine. Every now and then one of the old trees in the garden would come down in a long series of splintering cracks and a dull crash which shook the building.

'See everyone goes back to bed now,' Monsieur Brossay told Monsieur Sala. 'The planks'll hold all right. Anyway, the storm will be over by morning.'

Monsieur Boris staggered back from a brief inspection of the immediate vicinity.

'All's well with La Vallière,' he reported, 'except a dozen broken window-panes. But I didn't dare go farther. You can't walk; you have to go on hands and knees.'

There was no question of inspecting, there and then, the

damage to the empty wing on the other side of the courtyard. The headmaster sent Monsieur Juillet and the two Bretons back to bed and warned them to take care. Then he gathered the masters by the dormitory door and arranged with them to stay up while the storm lasted. They talked together in low voices while the evacuees remade their beds at the other end of the room.

Monsieur Brossay was leaning carelessly against the end partition. It was Chomel's. The trouble-maker of Le Plessis pretended to be fast asleep, his face buried in his pillow, his eyes tight shut and the bedclothes round his ears. But really he was frightened to death about his two thunder-flashes. What had happened to them in all the confusion? Had some Heaven-directed foot stamped on the fuse that smoked its snaky way to Monsieur Sala's corner? A jelly of fear, Chomel stealthily peered at his wrist-watch: eleven-fifty. 'I'm in the clear now,' he sighed to himself with relief.

At that very moment a shattering explosion lifted his mattress and deposited him on the floor, gasping like a fish out of water. The gale which raged outside was drowned in a roar of laughter. Chomel was a pitiable sight as in his crumpled pyjamas he got unsteadily to his feet and gaped, green with fright, at Monsieur Brossay, Monsieur Sala, Monsieur Boris and Monsieur Lacour, who were ranged like judges behind the partition.

'Corporal punishment is against school rules,' thundered the headmaster. 'But I shall see that this is the one exception which the school will always remember. Give me a slipper and bend over!'

Six whacks resounded to the delight of the dormitory.

'That's the first time I've seen you laugh,' Monsieur Boris murmured to little Monsieur Sala, when the excitement had subsided. 'You should do it more often. With a smile like that you could have tamed these young ruffians.'

'I'll remember that for my next job,' the other answered.

Nearby the lights of La Vallière went on one by one in the darkness as Monsieur Simon took Vignoles and Muret with him on a methodical tour of inspection. Jeantet was the only one who had been hurt, and lightly at that. He and Dubourg senior had an attic room on the second floor. The noise of the gale had woken them and they had opened the window to get a ringside view. Out of nowhere flew an old jam-tin to catch the bellman of Château-Milon a smack in the face. Charpenne was busy dabbing iodine on his nose. The main dormitory had suffered from a hail of missiles and the broken panes were stopped with sheets of cardboard and plywood.

Soon Monsieur Simon switched off the ceiling lights, but nobody went back to sleep in the smaller rooms. The gale continued to howl round the buildings with a strength which made sleep impossible. Picard was the only one to snore through it all, oppressed by the weight of his record-breaking meal.

At one o'clock in the morning, just as the gusts of wind began to grow less frequent, came the first power failure. All the lights went out together and the courtyard and the buildings round it were plunged in darkness. Vignoles, as he sat on the end of his bed, could see the wave of blackness surge across the window.

'Shall we have a light?' Charpenne asked from the other end of the room. 'I've got a packet of candles in my drawer.'

'You take good care of them,' Vignoles whispered back. 'If you ask me we're nowhere near out of the wood yet.'

He said no more, but got back into bed. In the next half-hour the wind gradually fell away and finally died out altogether. And then came the rain – unbroken, heavy, steady, filling the countryside with the dull roar of a waterfall. It was this continuous background music which finally sent them all to sleep, even Monsieur Sala, who was already thinking of the small suitcase he would have to pack, the books which would weigh so heavily and the good-byes which would be so embarrassing.

When at last day dawned it was upon a ravaged world half lost behind a curtain of rain. The courtyard had been turned from the beauty of St Martin's summer to a shambles. Water lapped at the litter of broken wood, bits of fencing, wisps of hay, a dead chicken and the hundred and one pieces of wreckage swept in from the fields around them.

The boys were soaked by their short journey to breakfast in the dining-hall. Monsieur Brossay had to confine them to their houses. Things, however, must have been better on the other side of the Loire, for Cunault Football Club rang the school in the morning to ask if the game was still on.

'Lend us a boat!' was Muret's answer as he hung up angrily.

Charpenne was in his seventh heaven with fifty-two others to share his detention. Monsieur Brossay took advantage of a slight slackening of the rain to run his wife and daughter into Angers by car. He came back before lunch to say that there seemed to be no dangerous developments, although the farmlands were ruined. The gale of the night before had destroyed nearly three thousand acres of orchard. Two barns had blown down at La Bohalle, and an old tenement on the outskirts of Angers had collapsed like a pack of cards, blocking the main road. The Loire had changed colour. Its sandbanks were now covered and the fishermen's punts between the bank and the Îles de Blaison had vanished in the storm.

'You'll only have a rather dull Sunday to get through,' Monsieur Brossay told the seniors. 'Once the weather clears I'll cut down the form-work so that you can make up for the fresh air you've lost.'

The real beneficiary of the disaster was undoubtedly Father Fabien, for the little chapel was packed to the doors for Mass. At half past twelve Jeantet, wearing his wounded face like a medal, opened the enormous umbrella Monsieur Juillet had lent him and made his stately way to Mérovée's Tower. He seized the bell-rope and Cunégonde rang clear and seemed to put new life into the broken routine of the school. All the same, the boys found the afternoon endless, imprisoned as they were by heavy driving rain which poured from a grey sky as though it would never stop. Monsieur Sala was hardly to be seen, either in his house or in the main building. Now that the little man had had his dismissal he kept discreetly out of the way as a prelude to his complete disappearance.

Just before supper, as night fell, the rain stopped abruptly. But the calm was all too short. As they were munching Madame Juillet's almond tarts the gale sprang up again with a force which drove them from their seats. They left the dining-hall in such confusion that Monsieur Brossay and the other masters had to shout above the storm to shepherd them together as they scattered in the darkness. The ever-obliging Monsieur Boris was with Monsieur Sala when he called the roll in the hallway of Le Plessis. There were no absentees. He followed them upstairs, after making sure that all the windows were secure and the door firmly shut. During the day Monsieur Juillet had been round to put a wooden cover over the broken window and to strengthen its neighbours. The wind could batter and howl, but they felt safe in the big dormitory, where a chastened Chomel sought refuge in sleep with the other frightened juniors. Rabbits' Eggs closed his two suitcases, set his alarm, tried a shy smile on his shaving-mirror and went to bed earlier than usual to enjoy the best night he had spent at Château-Milon – and his last. He was already asleep when the gale died down, and he never heard the rain approach the school and gradually possess the country for fifty miles around.

It was raining so hard the next morning that Jeantet did not have to be told not to go out to ring the getting-up bell. As usual Monsieur Sala took his charges down to the prep-room and left them in shivering silence in the half-light that filtered through the windows. The second storm had caused another power failure and the current had still not been re-established. The dismissed master went outside almost immediately to take a look at the headmaster's house. The wrath of the elements may sometimes soften the hardest of hearts and he half hoped Monsieur Brossay might have relented. But no, the Citröen Deux Chevaux belonging to the school was parked outside the front door as the head-master had instructed and Monsieur Juillet was waiting to drive him to the station.

There were no prolonged farewells. The weather was too poor for either pleasantry or sympathy, and when Monsieur Sala had loaded his luggage and turned again to Le Plessis there was not a face at the windows. He was forgotten al-ready. The car slowly crossed the courtyard, gradually vanishing in a sea of yellow mud. The gates were open. The rain veiled the countryside and the bucketing car soon disappeared down the narrow road to La Bohalle.

Half an hour later the boys were processing in gloomy silent file in their overcoats towards the dining-hall. They passed close against the front of the headmaster's house. Monsieur Brossay had come out under the front-door porch to watch them go by. He was getting rather worried: none of his day-boys had put in an appearance so far.

'This appalling weather's bound to delay everyone,' old Monsieur Corzon was saying as he stood beside him.

At last a car turned in at the gate, showering through the puddles. They turned to see who it was. But it was only the school's Deux Chevaux with Monsieur Juillet at the wheel and Monsieur Sala cowering behind the windscreen. The driver pulled up by the front door and stuck a worried face out of the window.

'Can't get through!' he called to Monsieur Brossay. 'The road's completely under water between Belle-Noue and La Bohalle. We'd only gone a mile when it was up to our hub-caps!'

Madame Brossay, her daughter and Father Fabien, had joined the other two at the front door. The news left them speechless. The headmaster hurried down the steps.

'You should have taken the long way round La Ménitré. The road along the embankment is bound to be all right.'

'It's even worse that way!' Monsieur Juillet answered with a gesture of defeat.

'How do you know?'

'I've just seen a farmer from Belle-Noue who'd tried it. In a couple of hours the Authion burst its banks along three miles and all the country's under water as far as Saint-Clément.'

'Well, that means we're in for it!' said Monsieur Brossay. 'And it doesn't look as though the rain's going to let up.'

The late-comers ran for the dining-hall, jumping the puddles in their path. Monsieur Brossay walked back to the porch with Monsieur Juillet, bustled the others indoors and stopped a moment in the doorway to discuss with his handy-man the steps they would have to take to meet this new emergency. As they turned to face the courtyard they eventually noticed little Monsieur Sala standing at the foot of the steps, like a piece of jetsam, firmly holding a suitcase in each hand. His thin face and enormous glasses were lost below his rain-soaked hat.

'What shall *I* do?' he asked bewilderedly.

In the state of the weather and the state of the roads his question bordered upon impertinence and Monsieur Brossay was too worried to check his retort.

'Do you want to swim away?'

Rabbits' Eggs tried to smile to hide his embarrassment. He was careful not to answer.

'Stay, of course! That's all you can do,' Monsieur Brossay went on impatiently. 'We'll see later. . .'

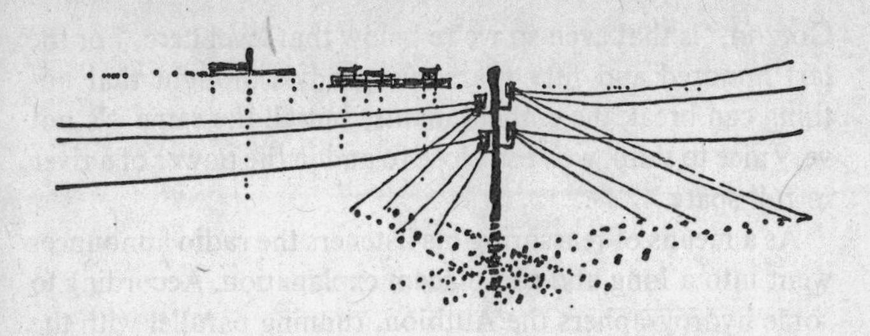

3 Monsieur Sala returned to his desk in the form-room of Le Plessis with new-found confidence and a secret glee which made his dark eyes shine behind their thick-lensed spectacles. He should have been thrown into panic by what he had just seen on his short journey. But it had had the effect of creating in him a surprising courage and the conviction that crises can sometimes be to the advantage of the weak and the despised. At least two feet of water covered the countryside and had stopped the Deux Chevaux a mile from Château-Milon. Under the dark and lowering sky the flat grey mass of water, broken only by scattered farm buildings, gate-posts or clumps of trees, took on a heart-wringing pathos. In the almost lazy way in which it had covered those familiar fields lay the threat of worse to follow.

Father Fabien had to leave his philosophy class to help Monsieur Brossay with his advice on what they should do to meet the emergency. Between telephone calls to the local authorities and to the school's suppliers they were able to pick up the weather forecasts for the area from the radio station at Nantes. These reports were so clearly designed to reassure that the threatened areas were only vaguely mentioned. The announcer implied that the floods would soon go down, since no danger threatened from the Loire, which had barely reached its spring flood-level.

'What the fool forgets to mention,' grumbled Monsieur

Corzon, 'is that even so we're below that level here. For the last hundred and fifty years everybody's thought that nothing can break the embankments, but all the same it's not very nice to think we're so close to and in the power of a river in full spate.'

As a means of reassuring his listeners the radio announcer went into a long and complacent explanation. According to some hydrographers the Authion, running parallel with the Loire between Saumur and Angers, was a natural outfall for that river. In the last thirty-six hours all the rain falling in the hinterland had poured into it and the suddenness of the first storm and the persistence of the downpour had resulted in a quantity of water in excess of the amount with which the fall of the river – barely six feet in thirty-six miles between Saumur and Les Ponts-de-Cé – could cope. It was only a matter of hours before the floods would go down. Better weather was forecast for that evening.

Meanwhile, continued the announcer, there was nothing to cause concern except serious damage to property and the difficulty of communication within the area Beaufort-Longué-Saint Clément-La Bohalle.

Monsieur Brossay sighed and switched off the radio.

'That means we're trapped in Château-Milon!' There was an edge to his voice.

'What are you worried about?' asked Father Fabien.

'I'm not anxious about food supplies. The Juillets have enough for another week. But we don't know how long the emergency may last. Then there are so many imponderables. We are on the knife-edge of disaster; it seems to be typical of the age we live in...'

'Cheer up! Don't be gloomier than those people!' Father Fabien gestured at the radio. 'Are you upset because your day-boys haven't turned up? I shouldn't complain if I were you. They're perfectly safe at home. If they were here they'd only be a further source of worry and responsibility and you'd have anxious parents ringing you up all the time!'

Madame Brossay and her daughter sat and listened to the two men. Edith's return to her boarding-school in Nantes had been postponed indefinitely. She was careful not to show how pleased she was. At seventeen it was fun to be thrown into something that smacked of adventure with plenty of males to share it.

Outside, as the rain came pelting down, hurried footsteps pattered along the terrace and Vignoles in a long black waterproof and gumboots stood dripping in the doorway.

'The flood's rising, Monsieur Brossay,' he said calmly. 'I've been to the end of the garden. The Authion's overflowed. Half the pitch is under water.'

His news fell like a thunder-clap. For ten seconds all that could be heard was the dull drumming of the downpour on the roofs and windows of Château-Milon.

'Impossible!' Monsieur Corzon exclaimed at last. 'They said it was clear that side an hour ago.'

'The water's rising ten times faster here than it is in the radio station,' Vignoles answered coldly.

'I'm coming,' Monsieur Brossay grunted.

Hurriedly he put on his waterproof, slipped into gumboots and went out on the heels of his pupil. They had to dodge their way down the garden path amid a litter of broken branches. When they reached the back gate Monsieur Brossay could hardly believe his eyes. The water stretched to the dark wooded hump of La Noue on the northern horizon. The trees that lined the banks of the Authion were scarcely visible. The whole vast stretch of water was alive with a current that swirled a pathetic mass of wreckage on its surface – hen-coops, hutches, dog kennels and dead animals turning slowly as the wind caught them. The flood now covered the games field to within fifty yards of the garden wall. Only the goalposts gave some slight indication as to where the football pitch had been.

'Look how it's rising.' Vignoles pointed.

They both floundered on the soggy turf and halted at the water's edge. For quite a while Monsieur Brossay stood in silence, his eyes fixed on the sullen tide advancing upon his property. Then they were forced back by the water, which snaked its way forward between the tussocks of grass.

'Well, the courtyard's just six feet above the level of the upper end of the playing-fields,' Monsieur Brossay murmured as if to himself.

'That's not much,' Vignoles observed.

'Yet it would take an awful lot of water to cover the ten-mile stretch on this side. The garden walls are firm. If we could block the gateway it would give us something to play with.'

'The seniors are itching to help,' Vignoles answered.

Monsieur Brossay was struck by the feeling behind the boy's words.

'I thought you didn't like Château-Milon,' he said gently.

'I've changed my mind since last night,' Vignoles retorted in his most icy tones.

Monsieur Brossay did not press him. Despite the fact that he had been treated as one of the headmaster's family during the long time he had been there, Vignoles had remained almost a stranger to him, enclosed in a wall of introspection which resisted all approaches. So instead of asking further questions he merely said, 'Let's find Monsieur Juillet at once!'

It had gone noon and half the school was still busy digging up the basket-ball pitch to fill the hundred or so sandbags they needed to make if they were to dam the breach of the garden gate. Vignoles, Muret and Picard, being the strongest, were on duty the whole time with heavily-laden wheelbarrows. Monsieur Juillet and the Trévidic brothers, helped by the younger masters, worked at the dam. Monsieur Brossay directed operations.

And still the waters rose. By lunchtime they had reached the foot of the dam. But it was solid and now rose head-high on broad, firmly-based foundations. The goalposts were half under water and the line of willows along the Authion had completely vanished. As far as the eye could see the fields behind the school were flooded. The oily yellow water swirled impatiently as the currents moved.

'We'll have to keep a constant watch on this side,' Monsieur Brossay decided. The speed and scope of the disaster had impressed him. 'It only needs a sudden rise in level for the situation to change in a matter of minutes.'

They arranged a rota and everyone left for lunch except Yvon Trévidic, who stood on guard under Monsieur Juillet's enormous umbrella. Lunch itself showed small sign that their supplies had been cut off. The dining-hall was more lively than usual, the boys light-hearted even. Now that the timetable of lessons had been partially abandoned, discipline relaxed. The presence of a danger which did not affect their personal well-being, excited them in an odd way. It was almost like Christmas Eve. The juniors had been confined to their house and they looked longingly at the dam-builders and eagerly questioned them about the progress of the floods.

'How did they behave themselves?' Monsieur Lacour asked. 'I hope they didn't give you too much trouble.'

'None so far,' little Monsieur Sala answered, with a smile which was becoming less and less forced. 'I've been sitting them up in my desk in turn and making them read two or three pages of *The Three Musketeers*. We've got as far as the breakfast with Aramis's friend, the old priest. If we go on to

Twenty Years After and *The Vicomte de Bragelonne* we've enough to keep us happy for another week.'

'Chomel, too?' Monsieur Boris asked laughingly.

'Chomel, too! He read the chapter about the duel in the Pré-aux-Clers all by himself.'

'What happened?'

'They ragged him as they never ragged me,' was the little man's delighted answer. 'I must say a real ragging isn't at all bad, if you're on the right side of it.'

'That's the spirit!' said Monsieur Lacour. 'You've got more grip on them in the last two hours than you've had in the previous two months.'

Rabbits' Eggs nodded. There was the slightest trace of disappointment on his face.

'I'd much rather be helping you.'

'Your turn will come sooner than you think,' Monsieur Boris gravely assured him.

The three ceiling lights and the wall lights, which they had had to switch on at noon, suddenly went out, plunging the dining-hall into semi-darkness. It was the third failure since the night of the gale. It was also the last; Château-Milon was to be without electricity from now on.

Between two and three that afternoon it brightened slightly, though the sun did not break through. On guard at the dam were Vignoles and the soft-skinned Vicomte Boisson de Chazelles, muffled in an elegant, fur-trimmed duffle-coat and complaining all the time of the cold. They watched a flat muddy sea stretching to the horizon and reflecting a watery sky across which galloped a black cavalry of clouds.

The goalposts were completely covered. The water was half-way up the walls and within two feet of the top of the dam. Every so often it would seep through the sandbags, to be absorbed by the clay they contained.

'Hurry and tell Monsieur Brossay.' Vignoles turned to his companion. 'We need to raise the dam a good three feet. If the water goes on rising at this rate all night, the garden will be a quagmire by tomorrow and the floods'll be coming in at the back door.'

The work of reinforcement proceeded in orderly fashion, but with a haste and energy which now betrayed their fear. Monsieur Brossay brought in the juniors to help the diggers feverishly filling sandbags. The seniors ran with their wheelbarrows to the end of the garden, where Monsieur Juillet and the two Bretons were working in the gateway like men possessed in order to finish before nightfall.

By half past four Monsieur Brossay decided there was little more they could usefully do. The dam filled the gateway to the top of the walls on either side. Monsieur Boris and the burly Picard stayed on guard at the foot of the ladders resting against the sandbags. These were stacked regularly against the gate, like the piles of a bridge, to plug the weakest point in the wall round the school. But it was really only the flimsiest of defences. Fortunately, though, the waters seemed now to have reached their peak, or to be rising so slowly as to give no grounds for concern. Monsieur Lacour expressed in an undertone the feelings of several of his pupils.

'I'd feel a lot happier if we could do the same all round the grounds. One crack between these old stones and the weight of water will bring a whole length of wall crashing down. Then we'll have to swim for it if we want to cross the courtyard.'

Monsieur Brossay stayed behind with Vignoles and Monsieur Juillet. Then they, too, strode back in gloomy conversation. As they reached the corner of his house the headmaster heard his telephone ringing and hurried away. Vignoles and Monsieur Juillet went on to the far end of the courtyard to see what progress the floods had made on the southern front of Château-Milon. Nothing seemed to have changed in the immediate vicinity, the water still lapped at the slight rise in the land which carried a dozen scattered farms and the narrow road to La Bohalle.

Beyond lay the unknown. As night fell it mingled still water and sodden ground in the same twilit uncertainty. In the distance two objects stood out above the chaos, the line of the embankment, running across the country like an extra horizon, and the lonely shoulder of the Arcy woods, seemingly much closer than it really was. They could see tiny points of light moving about on it. Monsieur Juillet scanned the horizon with his field-glasses. Momentarily he picked out two large flat-bottomed boats slipping past, packed with people. Although he did not mention it, the sight sent a cold shiver down his spine.

Vignoles had turned automatically to stare at the buildings round the courtyard. He was looking up and seemed to be measuring their height and then looking away to judge it by comparison with the lie of the land. Monsieur Juillet guessed what he was thinking. He was a local man and a mine of local history.

'At the moment,' he said in a low voice, 'we're nearly surrounded by water. At any minute now we could be in deadly danger from both sides at once. You're wondering what use this foothold'll be if the floods go on rising and if the Loire should suddenly spill over the embankment? Well, there'd be one big lake fifteen miles wide from Fontaine-Guérin to Saint-Rémy-La Varenne on the other side of the Loire.'

'What makes you say that?' the astonished Vignoles asked.

'Well, that's what happened in the big floods in 1820,' Monsieur Juillet answered. 'I can show you old accounts of it any time you like. The only things above water, between Angers and Saumur were the Arcy woods . . . and the top of Mérovée's Tower!'

Vignoles turned and stared up at the old mill with its round slate roof rising sixty feet above him.

'Gospel truth,' Monsieur Juillet went on. 'If Monsieur Brossay let you boys inside the ruin I could show you a funny sort of calendar cut into one of the roof beams. Mérovée, his wife and his man were cut off by the floods and spent a week perched up among the beams and cog-wheels with only a pair of owls and a dozen rats for company. The mill is a mill no more, but she still keeps the name of her last miller.'

To Charpenne life at Château-Milon had all the magic of the Castle of the Lake in the *Morte d'Arthur*. He was Lancelot and wherever he turned in this enchanted place there was his Guinevere in white raincoat and little rubber boots. Edith Brossay could not bear the mournful sitting-room on the ground floor and was to be seen everywhere, smiling encouragement and helping with even the most unpleasant tasks.

As Lancelot was piling earth into an old sack his hand chanced upon another anxious to help him. He turned to find himself face to face with the young enchantress who had already cost him eight hours' detention, seven bars of chocolate and last but not least five brain-racking sonnets. His sixth was in his pocket. It was all, or nearly all, his own work. Whether it was any better than the others can be left to the reader's judgement.

> The wind of Death's imperishable wing
> Has brushed my brow, but may Fate's stroke be stay'd
> Until the piteous song which now I sing,
> Edith, has touched your heart, hard-hearted maid.

Upon the beached verge of the salt flood
As it descends, in Château-Milon's gutter
You'll find my heart. The song birds of the wood
Shall sing my love which now offends to utter.
Fly then to cloudless climes and starry skies!
Thy beauty 'scapes and laughs to see my eyes
Drop tears. Into Death's fatal bark I go
Alone. Unless by Fate the floods shall flow
Over us both. At last in death us join
Your Romeo, I, and you sweet Juliet, mine.

Charpenne fumbled in his pocket and pressed a muddy piece of paper upon Edith. Then to hide his hope and his embarrassment he fled down the garden path as if the Devil himself were behind him. He ran straight into little Jozas, who had just come out of the garage with an armful of empty sacks.

'Any messages?' he asked. 'Supplies are short, so I've cut my rates to half a bar.'

'You're too late in the day!' Charpenne called as he hurried past. 'From now on I'm doing my own dirty work!'

The rain came down again and the gale sprang up. The gusts boomed like gun-fire among the roof-tops. Monsieur Brossay had set up his command post in the drawing-room of his house. By the light of an aged acetylene lamp he wrestled with the telephone in an attempt to get through to Angers and Saumur for news. Darkness and storm pricked the bubble of courage and high spirits which had kept seniors and juniors going all day. They clustered round Monsieur Lacour's transistor set. The announcers, with no overall picture of the situation, went on with their hourly bulletins whose optimism made the listeners smile. Vignoles brought the only encouraging news on one of his many trips between school and garden wall.

'The floods from the Authion have only risen an inch or

two in the last three hours,' he told the silent circle. 'Monsieur Boris has been inspecting the wall foot by foot and no water is seeping through. We did find it coming through a rabbit-hole in the northern corner by the woodshed, but we soon blocked it up. The sandbags seem to be holding all right, but the flood-level is only two feet below the top of our dam.'

He was addressing a full battle group of the school, Father Fabien, the Bursar, Monsieur Juillet, three of the other masters and the five most senior boys. Monsieur Brossay now gave them a résumé of the situation from the information he had gleaned from radio bulletins and telephone calls.

'We are not the only ones cut off and battling against disaster. Thousands of homes in the area are faced by the same dangers. The Civil Defence teams are already overwhelmed by calls for help. In normal times their resources in men and materials are limited, and in an emergency they have to be reinforced by troops, police and firemen. But they need a week to rally these forces and make their use effective. No one could foresee the extent or speed of the disaster. While they fear the worst, they drum into us that there is still no real threat. However, we are in too dangerous a position to believe that. The best thing we can do is take precautions for this very night.'

The first need was to organize a continuous guard on the dam and a group in the headmaster's house permanently on watch and ready to meet any emergency. Monsieur Brossay decided to take charge of this second party, which was to comprise, in addition to himself, Monsieur Juillet and the Trévidic brothers. As for the guards, they would make their tours of duty in pairs. Thus there would have to be twelve of them to provide reliefs every two hours. Further, each pair would have to be a physically balanced team. First, then,

Montaigu was crossed off the list as being too young and not having the physique. Monsieur Boris chose Muret, whose quick wits and cool head were not confined to the football field, while Monsieur Simon took the young Vicomte under his wing. Hubert Boisson de Chazelles found the atmosphere 'rather agreeable. This disaster, don't you know, and the school like an armed camp.' Monsieur Lacour could not but choose Guillon, his star mathematician; when they tried to dissuade Father Fabien because of his age and his rheumatism, the priest protested so strongly that they had to put him on first watch with Lalande to partner him. Stolid Picard and Charpenne were together, although the latter was spiritually miles away from Château-Milon. This left Vignoles on his own. They needed one other to make up the round dozen. Then they realized Monsieur Sala was not there. For the last few hours he had taken on the task single-handed of keeping happy those with no duties to perform.

'Do you think he'll do it?' Monsieur Brossay asked Vignoles.

'I'm sure he will.'

The headmaster turned to Monsieur Simon.

'Tell him at dinner. If he hedges we'll take Jeantet.'

Monsieur Sala's slender frame had been considered too slight for the toils of dam-building, but his setting them to read had at least kept under shelter a group of juniors for whom it would have been dangerous had they been allowed to run wild in the pouring rain. Gradually the seniors had drifted into the form-room of Le Plessis until both houses filled it. In the flickering candlelight Cardinal Richelieu was berating d'Artagnan in Kiki Dubourg's treble. An enthusiastic audience was reacting with the same fervour they would have shown to a cowboy film. The youthful reader was perched up in the master's desk and every time a horse galloped through the story his heels spurred the empty air as the room dissolved in laughter. Monsieur Sala smiled as he walked between the desks with his hands behind his back. A nod of his head regulated the din and his happiness was plain to see. As he walked unobserved behind a group of seniors at the back of the form-room he had heard one of them say to his neighbour:

'*Monsieur* Sala was a dark horse!'

'Rabbits' Eggs' died in that moment and the stupid nickname was forgotten for ever. The little man gently patted Chomel's shoulder as he passed. He bore him no ill will, but the boy never looked up. His long goat-like face was even more pasty than usual and provided the one point of gloom in the cheerful audience.

Little Jozas seemed the happiest of them all. He had had a wonderful day. When the poet of the Sixth had dismissed him so abruptly his luck had led him at once to the basket-ball pitch, where Mademoiselle Edith had just finished filling a sandbag. The sixth and last sonnet had touched the school's enchantress as none of its predecessors had done.

'Run off to the kitchen! Hurry up and bring me back the other notes. Yes, I want them all!'

Fortunately Madame Juillet had kept these strange effusions under a mustard-pot. She had other things to think about and made no objection to his taking them away. So while Jozas delightedly patted pockets stuffed with chocolate from the headmaster's private store, Edith sat in her little room, oblivious even of the gale raging outside. One by one she read 'her' sonnets, acknowledged the lines lifted here from Ronsard, here from Lamartine, there from some other great poet, and howled with laughter at the heart in the gutter. Sympathy and then friendship made her read and re-read Charpenne's poor plagiarized verses.

Dinner was earlier than usual and, of course, by candle-light. But that was enough to lend an air of festivity to the meal. There was less to eat than usual and it came out of tins. Monsieur Simon had passed Monsieur Brossay's message to his friend, Monsieur Sala, telling him he was quite free to refuse to do guard duty if he wished.

Vignoles kept a close, if discreet, eye on the masters' table, but he could not make out if he had accepted. However, on several occasions he caught Monsieur Sala's glasses flashing in his direction, the same glasses which had often made the little master look stupid and turned the silliness of some of the boys to ragging. In two months the new master and Château-Milon's oldest inhabitant had merely passed the time of day. At first Vignoles had remained honestly indifferent, but then the fact that everyone stubbornly persecuted the wretched man awoke his sympathy. Their duty that night seemed designed for him to discover what went on behind those heavy spectacles.

As he was leaving the dining-hall and edging past the groups that shouted to one another in the darkness he felt Monsieur Sala's gentle tap on his elbow.

'Where shall we meet?' he asked uncertainly.

'It's our bad luck to have the worst tour of duty – from two to four in the morning. Stay in Le Plessis until it's time to go on watch and try to get some sleep. I'll pick you up on my way from La Vallière.'

'Can I do anything to help in the meantime?'

'Put on your warmest clothes, that's all. Don't bother about a torch. I've got a big one and we needn't be afraid of using it as much as we want. All the rest's plain sailing if there are the two of us and we keep our eyes open and don't get the wind up no matter what happens.'

Monsieur Sala went on with conventional politeness.

'So you think something *will* happen tonight?'

Vignoles glanced round to make sure that no one could overhear him.

'I'm certain it will.'

He made no attempt to dominate the little man, and had only spoken with the detachment and confidence of an old hand who knew the school and the country round it, but the latter seemed instinctively to put himself under his orders.

Monsieur Sala's glasses glittered in the darkness.

'What makes you so sure?'

'I've been tramping the grounds for the last two days,' Vignoles went on quietly. 'I know I've never seen a flood before, but when you've watched every detail of a disaster there are some signs which are unmistakable. One thing alone could have saved this corner of the valley, if the weather had cleared at lunchtime and the rain had stopped. It's too late now. Nothing can hold back the floods.'

4 At ten o'clock that night the wind dropped. The last gusts blew themselves out in the distance. It was so sudden that the whole countryside seemed to have slipped into a vacuum. Then the rain came down as heavily as it had that morning and the night was full of its monotonous swish. The dull soporific sound wrapped the school, its buildings, grounds and courtyard in a blanket of softness and peace which gave the inmates a false sense of security. Those who were on watch in the headmaster's house, at the dam and in the senior house had to fight a deadly lassitude.

The individual rooms in La Vallière were served by a staircase separate from the dormitory, and now they were a strange sight with their doors left open, the candlelight flickering and leaving great patches of shadow. There was a continual whispering and pattering of feet as the boys, who were neither able nor wanting to sleep, passed from one to another. Lalande had just come off guard and he shivered under the black oilskins Vignoles had lent him.

'What's the news?' someone called to him from the shadows.

'No change!' he said and snorted. 'Or very little: about six inches in two hours. But the water's up to this afternoon's work and there's only about eighteen inches clear.'

'At that rate,' said Picard, 'the crash'll come around dawn. Who'll be on then?'

'Vignoles and little Monsieur Sala,' Charpenne answered.

Vignoles was lying fully dressed on his bed and sleeping, or pretending to.

'How did it go?' Muret asked Lalande. 'Not too tough?'

'I'm not complaining. Father Fabien kept me warm for the two hours with his stories about Africa and China. We nearly died of laughing.'

Hubert Boisson de Chazelles had just gone on duty with Monsieur Simon.

'I can hear his teeth chattering from here!' Lalande chuckled. 'It'll take our noble lord a week to get over this lot. You should have seen him come tiptoeing across the muck trailing his umbrella. It would have killed you!'

Montaigu had no set duty to perform that night, so he undertook cook-house fatigue and warmed a saucepan of cocoa over the flame of a candle. Lalande was given the first cup, but Picard scented it and came up with nostrils flared to ask for his share there and then.

'I'd like to,' said the cook, 'but you'll really need something inside you when you come off guard.'

Charpenne thought gloomily of his Edith. The sixth sonnet had misfired badly, for it was surely poor taste to trifle on the brink of disaster.

'What'll happen if the water floods into the garden?' he asked them all.

Muret shrugged despondently.

'We had a good look this afternoon with Monsieur Lacour. At the danger-point the garden walls are exactly on a level with the courtyard. So the flooding wouldn't be catastrophic. We'd just get our feet wet when we went from one building to another. Then the road to La Bohalle is on an embankment, so it will be clear to the Arcy woods. But after that the slightest worsening in the situation will make things really tough for us. The more the water rises the more we shall be cut off. If we look on the black side and assume we stay here, our only protection will be two floors and an attic... What will Monsieur Brossay decide tomorrow? What happens tonight will settle that.'

A moment's silence greeted his calm revelations. Muret was so sensible and level-headed. Then Charpenne threw himself on his bed.

'I don't believe you!' he suddenly burst out. 'Things'll never get as bad as that.'

Just before midnight Vignoles woke with a start as a series of shattering explosions rattled the window-panes. Simultaneously a red glow flickered in the darkness and lit the distant embankment with its string of white houses. The boys rushed to the windows. It had stopped raining in the last ten minutes. All around it had cleared and there was the same sort of pale shimmer that can be seen on the open sea.

Scarcely twenty seconds later and once more the sky was lit up. There was time to see the church at La Ménitré, the sloping Arcy woods and the few islanded acres of dry land which seemed to float on the floods.

Then the long boom of the explosion re-echoed from horizon to horizon.

'That's from La Bohalle,' Guillon muttered, his nose squashed against the panes. 'But the first one was much farther over to the right.'

Vignoles opened the window and leaned out. Someone was coming down the steps of the headmaster's house and splashing heavily through the puddles. He recognized Monsieur Juillet, his silhouette thickened by his hooded oilskins.

'What can you see from up there?' he called anxiously.

At that moment there was a blinding flash that lit up all the country to the west. The thick ceiling of low cloud and the crooked curtain of a rainstorm glowed nearby. The boom of the explosion died away.

'That was dynamite.' Monsieur Juillet was emphatic. 'If you ask me they've blown something upstream from Angers.'

He half-turned and his hooded figure was lost in the darkness of the courtyard. A few minutes later Boisson de Chazelles came off duty with confirmation of the news. He and Monsieur Simon had just been relieved by Monsieur Boris and Muret. Everyone expected the Vicomte to be unnerved by his ordeal, but he came through the doorway with a victorious expression on his face, mud up to his thighs and his elegant duffle-coat obstinately worn despite the soaking weight of two hours' rain.

'We came through the headmaster's house to report to him,' he told them. 'Monsieur Brossay was just on the line to the town hall at Longué. The troops are blowing a quarter-mile gap in the embankment. The floods from the Authion are threatening Angers.'

'That's a stupid thing to do!' Charpenne said dully.

'Oh no, it's not,' Hubert retorted. 'At the moment the Loire is running ten feet below flood-level. In a few hours all the water round us will have been drained into it.'

'Things must have got pretty bad downstream for them to have sacrificed their defence deliberately,' Vignoles sighed. 'The old embankment was originally built along a twenty-five mile stretch to hold the Loire in check, and all it has done is to end up by drowning the countryside it was intended to protect. Of course, a freak storm makes a difference. They thought the danger would come from the Loire and it has come from the Authion instead. Three days' rain has turned the embankment into a death trap, and we and the five or six thousand others who are cut off are caught in it like rats. But just suppose the Loire goes on rising, as all the water that's fallen since Saturday drains into its basin. What'll happen then? Will they have time to close the breach? If the flood sweeps down suddenly the water that's lapping the garden wall now may well be swirling over the roof by tomorrow.'

For twenty minutes the explosions continued, rattling the panes of the windows and making the foundations shake.

No one slept in La Vallière, where they had a grandstand view from the window. The break in the weather had not lasted and the flashes from the final explosions were dimmed

by a curtain of rain. Every so often one of the boys would go to the head of the stairs to peer out into the darkness beyond the front windows.

'If the wall gives,' Lalande was saying, 'we'll soon know about it. The courtyard'll be under water in a matter of seconds. I hope the watchmen keep awake. Lucky for Boris and Muret they've the fastest pairs of legs in the school!'

At a quarter to two Vignoles slipped his oilskins over two thick sweaters, secured his powerful torch to his belt, smiled to the others and made for the staircase.

'Who's on with you?' Charpenne asked him.

'Monsieur Sala.'

'Keep an eye on him,' Picard joked. 'Watch out you don't get those sandbags on top of you. Your mate'll be washed away like a dead leaf!'

As he neared the neighbouring house Vignoles saw a stubby shape move from the entrance.

'I've been waiting for you,' murmured Monsieur Sala in the darkness. 'I couldn't get a wink of sleep.'

It was comic to see how he vanished under a raincoat sizes too big which Monsieur Simon had kindly lent him, while his face disappeared under his old hat with its floppy brim.

'Come on!' Vignoles said eagerly. 'We'll drop into the headmaster's house first before we relieve the others.'

On their way they met ghostly figures coming round the corner from the kitchen quarters, the water dripping from their coats. The Trévidic brothers were bent beneath huge loads.

'We're shifting the food supplies,' Job explained. 'The kitchens are too exposed.'

They had to raise their voices almost to a shout to make themselves heard above the unbroken drumming of the rain.

Monsieur Brossay's face was pale and strained as he conferred in the sitting-room with Monsieur Juillet and Father

Fabien, who sucked an empty pipe. He greeted the relief with an agonized smile.

'The position hasn't improved,' he told them. 'The water is still rising. Not so fast, of course, but down by the gate it has nearly reached the top of the dam formed by the garden walls. They didn't do much good with their dynamite. To have had any real effect on the floods they should have blown up four miles of embankment.'

In the smoky light of the acetylene lamp his voice was weary. He sat with arms crossed at his desk, the telephone on his right. The receiver was off and the cord trailed across a scattering of papers, as though it were something useless and unimportant. Monsieur Brossay caught Vignoles's curious glance.

'Now,' he admitted, 'we really are cut off. Up to a moment ago I could get through to the exchanges at Beaufort and Longué. Then within the last five minutes there was a click, and the line went dead. I can't get a sound out of it. Not being able to speak to the outside world is the worst part of being besieged like this.'

Monsieur Sala and Vignoles got their instructions from Monsieur Juillet and were just going out when Monsieur Brossay called them back.

'Keep a good look-out!' were his parting words. 'If the wall goes, run for it as hard as you can to my house.'

The watchmen plunged into the night. Before them the beam of the torch cut a glittering band through the rain.

The garden path was deep in mud and in some places they sank half-way to their knees. Most of the time they were forced to climb gingerly over fallen trees and to edge their way past the broken branches heaped up by the gale.

Every so often Vignoles would switch off his own torch in an endeavour to get his bearings from any torchlight there might have been by the gate. They could see nothing, and then the beam of his own torch glanced upon the mossy walls and the sandbags piled to fill the gateway. The two ladders leaning crookedly against the barrier just reached the top. There was nobody on the left-hand one, but at the top of the other a figure was perched, leaning on the sandbags and staring out at a horizon invisible from the ground.

It was Monsieur Boris. He straightened up when he heard their footsteps splashing behind him and swung the beam of his torch on the newcomers. The water seeping through the sandbags already formed a lake around the gateway.

'Where's Muret?' Vignoles asked anxiously.

'He's on patrol along the walls,' Monsieur Boris answered. 'In the last hour cracks have been starting to show all over the place. You want to watch out, with that tonnage of water pressing on our walls.'

'How high is it?'

'We've held it. Come and see.'

Vignoles buckled his torch to his belt and climbed the other ladder.

He shivered to see the black water so close and level with his shoulders. The flood bubbled in the driving rain and licked the last layer of sandbags, the rampart of their dam. This meant that for over a hundred yards the gardens were dominated by a motionless mass of water which stretched for miles beyond the few yards their torches showed them.

'It only needs one crack to widen,' Monsieur Boris said in a low voice, 'and the pressure'll do the rest. Down will go the wall and the water will come sweeping up the garden till it reaches the kitchens. From then on we'll be cut off separately in the headmaster's house, in Le Plessis, in La Vallière, everywhere. Has Monsieur Brossay told you what to do?'

'We must keep at least twenty yards away,' Vignoles answered. 'Preferably on the raised edge of the tennis courts so that we shan't be in danger if the wall goes suddenly.'

'He came down not so long ago,' Monsieur Boris went on gravely, 'and said the same thing to us. Muret and I may have taken no notice, but now, Vignoles, *I'm* telling you to keep clear. Take one more look at the flood so you remember what you've seen, get down the ladder and keep away from it.'

Muret came striding through the darkness, swinging his torch like a railway ganger.

'No change!' he called. 'A small piece of stone's come out of the top of the wall near the wood-pile. The water's spurting through like a fountain, but it's too late to do anything about it now. You've seen how it's been coming down!'

All four walked back to the tennis courts which, with the wire netting round them, dominated this part of the garden. Monsieur Boris handed his torch to Monsieur Sala and then, having warned them not to take any risks, he went off with Muret.

The first thing Vignoles did was to sweep the beam of his torch round in a wide arc. Thirty yards in front of them they could see the footing of sandbags with which the base of the wall had been strengthened. Beyond that the beam was lost in a tangle of waterlogged branches and shrubbery.

They walked over to the wall on their right and progressed along it, keeping their distance, to take a look at the fault which Muret had discovered. Six feet up, the water had forced a small slab out and jetted through horizontally, to thunder down into a pool which grew bigger as they watched it. But in the downpour this seemed a small threat.

They talked as they made their rounds. Monsieur Sala's tongue was loosened at long last and he laughed as he told the story of the cats, Saturday's monumental ragging and his sorry dismissal which resulted from it.

'If it had happened a day earlier,' Vignoles remarked, 'you'd have been out of the hole we're in now! Monsieur Brossay could just as well have sent you off on Sunday morning.'

'I'm glad he didn't,' was Monsieur Sala's spirited retort. 'You really live in an emergency!'

Vignoles nodded his hooded head.

'That's what I think,' he said softly. 'Up to now I've looked on Château-Milon as an exile. The gale on Saturday brought me to my senses. It's taken me six years to realize what the school means to each one of us: safety, order, a breathing-space before we go out into the world, a place where we can be happy, study and learn how to live with other people. When I came I had the bad luck to play up to the wrong set and win the disapproval of the decent sorts. But that's all over and done with and I need my friends around me as much as the air I breathe... Let's go back to the tennis courts.'

They resumed their watch on the outer wall, crossing and recrossing the raised hard courts which overlooked the garden gate. When half an hour had gone and still nothing had happened, the temptation proved too strong.

'What can you see from the top of the ladder?' Monsieur Sala suddenly asked him.

'Water!' Vignoles answered. 'You can even dip your fingers in it. The football pitch is flooded ten feet deep. You know that, it's nothing. Yet coming on it when you don't expect it you suddenly feel as though you are staring down into the Pacific.'

'Shall we have a look?' suggested Monsieur Sala.

The other was just going to ask the same question. Together they scrambled down the muddy steps from the hard courts and made for the gate. Before he even touched the ladder Vignoles knew that the end was at hand. The water lapped the parapet and had begun its slow, treacherous seepage over the top, down the rounded sides of the sandbags and into the quagmire at their feet.

They did not speak as they climbed and saw the vast lake stretched level with the walls and hanging there as if restrained by supernatural means. And yet a gust of wind, a wave or the shock of a piece of floating wreckage would have been enough to send it flooding over.

'I'd better warn Monsieur Brossay, don't you think?' said Monsieur Sala expressionlessly.

'Best thing. It's hopeless now and he could take steps to protect the school.'

Monsieur Sala climbed down carefully, as if one false step could unleash disaster.

When he reached the ground he seemed to hesitate.

'No nonsense, eh?' he called to Vignoles. 'If you hear anything give, beat it!'

He slithered away in the darkness.

Five minutes later Vignoles heard the faint sound of an engine revving up behind the buildings. The school had three vehicles – a Citröen van used for fetching the groceries, Monsieur Brossay's Citröen Deux Chevaux and his Peugeot 203. Normally they were garaged in an old barn by the kitchens. Now the headmaster was having them moved. Three times the courtyard was lit by the glare of headlights as Monsieur Juillet drove each vehicle successively out through the main gate and parked it on the road to La Bohalle, which was raised above the initial onslaught of the floods. The noise awoke the whole school and curious noses pressed against the dormitory windows. The rain was falling even more heavily and its hissing veil shrouded the grounds and made the night still darker.

Monsieur Sala was on the terrace awaiting further orders.

'Go and find Vignoles at once,' Monsieur Brossay called

as he came in. 'There is no point in taking unnecessary risks. Then go straight back to your houses. I don't want anyone to stay out of doors.'

The little man hurried off towards the garden. He splashed through the puddles which bubbled in the rain. Vignoles had not left his ladder. He leaned right over the parapet, literally hypnotized by the sight of the slumbering flood whose weight he could almost feel stirring against his body.

'Come down! Hurry! Let's get out of here!' Monsieur Sala shouted, wild with alarm.

Away to their left, there was a dull crash and then the drumming of the rain was drowned by a roaring which increased in volume and came from behind the trees. Vignoles reached the ground and shook his dripping waterproof. The noise had become so loud that they could hardly hear themselves speak.

'Wait for me by the corner of the hard courts,' he shouted to Monsieur Sala. 'I'm going down to see what's happened.'

He was off at once, holding his torch over his head. Thirty yards farther on he suddenly found the flood up to his knees. The water boiled over the fallen trees and swept through the shrubberies.

Vignoles struggled forward foot by foot against the current.

The beam from his torch swept from side to side, then suddenly focused. The boy stopped, his heart in his mouth. At the far end of the garden ten or fifteen feet of wall had caved in. Through the gap thundered a solid stream of swirling ice-grey water.

In the background Monsieur Sala's voice sounded feebly.

'Come back, Vignoles! Come back at once! We'll both be caught!'

Vignoles retraced his steps, fighting his way like a madman through the broken branches tangled across his path.

In several places the water was flooding over the top of the wall and bringing whole sections of it crashing down. As far as the eye could see the garden was under two feet of water.

Vignoles jumped for the hard courts. They were deserted.

'Where are you?'

As he turned he saw the flicker of Monsieur Sala's torch by the dam as he ran, his own pointed in that direction. Suddenly he could see the little man spreadeagled across the sandbags, trying with his feeble strength to restrain an ocean.

At the same time Vignoles could see the sinister shiver as the whole mass of the dam almost imperceptibly began to topple backwards.

'Have you gone mad?' he shouted. 'Get away!'

Furiously he tugged at Monsieur Sala's shoulders. They both fled for their lives. Thirty yards lay between them and the hard courts and then there were the steps to climb. Their feet were on the first of these when there was a crash that made the earth tremble and a stream of water came jetting from the gate and caught them between the shoulder blades. Vignoles heaved and hauled his companion to the plateau of the courts. They turned and switched on their torches.

The sandbag dam had given in one solid mass, opening the gardens to the flood. Directly before them and almost at their level a turbulent river flowed noisily in and spread out among the trees. In a few seconds the gate-posts were gone like melting snow under the tremendous pressure. Then there was a sinister crack as the whole wall shuddered and fell in a lump that broke to right and left as the water drove through.

In an instantaneous flash Monsieur Sala and Vignoles saw the wave hang ten feet high. They fled for the headmaster's house as fast as their legs could carry them. All round them the darkness was a confusion of gurgling, crashing, hissing water like the noise of the waves on a shelving beach. The flood gathered on the ground it had won, to sweep on to fresh conquests.

Monsieur Brossay was outside, standing on the terrace with Monsieur Juillet and the three masters as the watchmen ran past to their respective houses.

'Stay indoors!' the headmaster called to them.

The surge of the water could be heard quite clearly now in the school.

Monsieur Juillet leaned over the balustrade and shone his torch on to the gravel of the courtyard.

'This is it,' he sighed. 'Look!'

Two black sheets of water, pouring round each wing, flowed almost lazily together under the front door. The stealthy progress of the floods was now so threatening that the men shivered in silence for a moment or two as they gazed at the whorls and ripples on the surface.

'At the moment,' Monsieur Juillet grunted at last, 'it's only a foot deep, but will it rise? That's the question. If you ask me we ought sooner or later to feel the effect of breaching the embankment.'

No one took him up. He clumped down the steps to test the depth. Only the bottom two were under water.

'We'll see in a few hours. Meanwhile let's all get some sleep.' Monsieur Brossay was worn out.

The telephone was still out of action. From below came the muffled thunder of the water pouring into the cellars through imperfectly sealed air-holes. The clock in the sitting-room struck four. There was no lighting, no heating, and the headmaster's house was bitterly cold. It was even colder in Le Plessis, where, soaked to the skin and with his teeth chattering, Monsieur Sala stripped to change into the only dry clothes he had – his Sunday best.

On the first floor of La Vallière the seniors stood in a gossiping circle round Vignoles as he sipped a small cup of cocoa.

'I've got enough for another.' Montaigu held out the saucepan. 'Who wants it?'

Picard was reaching for it when one look from Vignoles stopped him short.

'Little Sala's got an empty belly,' he said harshly, 'and we caught the worst watch. If he doesn't crack up, he must be made of cast-iron. You take him the cocoa, he really has deserved it!'

All except Boisson de Chazelles were in varying stages of undress.

'You going?' Montaigu asked him. 'It's quite safe. The covered way is above the flood.'

'Perhaps it's beneath his dignity to be a waiter,' Charpenne teased the Vicomte.

Hubert shrugged and went downstairs with the steaming saucepan. That was the last they saw of him. He spent the rest of the night in Monsieur Sala's room astride a chair, arms on the back of it, head bent over a pocket chess-board the little man had unearthed. A passing reference to it had set them off. The Vicomte was a really good player, so was Monsieur Sala, and their game lasted until daybreak.

It was eight o'clock before a leaden light broke through the thick clouds. The rain had nearly stopped. There lay the courtyard under a shimmering sea of muddy water which surrounded the headmaster's house, La Vallière, Le Plessis and the classroom block above the dining-hall. It lapped the rocky mound on which stood Mérovée's Tower, spared the terrace chapel, but seeped over the tarmac drive which led to the road. In four hours the flood had risen a bare six inches: very little by comparison with its gains between midday and midnight of the day before.

This respite and the clearing of the rain were keenly debated in the headmaster's drawing-room by what was really a council of war whose members split into opposing factions: the optimists and the pessimists. Madame Brossay and Edith had just come in and their silent presence prevented the argument from becoming embittered. They had no telephone, they had no radio – Monsieur Lacour's set had broken down – and it was therefore difficult for anyone to base his opinion on the true facts of the disaster. Faced by something of which they could not foresee the outcome, they were all reduced to intuition or experience. Each in turn put his point of view and the reasons why he held it.

Monsieur Brossay let the others open the debate. The terrors of the night before still oppressed some. Father Fabien and Monsieur Juillet were the first to raise the question of evacuation, and *that* put the cat among the pigeons. Their escape route ran to the Arcy woods, but when they got there what living conditions and accommodation were they likely to find? Monsieur Boris and his friends were in agreement against moving and supported their viewpoint with practical considerations which could not be ignored. When, at last, everyone had had their say they looked to the master of Château-Milon.

Monsieur Brossay sat rigid in his chair, the picture of indecision. Deep down he felt forebodings of disaster, but it hurt him more than he would care to admit to think of uprooting his boys from their quarters and of throwing them into the mud and wind of a refugee camp in which perhaps a thousand people already crouched in waterlogged tents, fought for a crust of bread or a hot drink, and shivered in fever and despair.

Father Fabien tilted the scales.

'Don't trust in the false security of these walls,' he said cuttingly, 'and don't expect any outside aid at all. There should be one motive behind your decision: we have been entrusted with forty children and we are responsible for their safety. No one will blame you if you have been overscrupulous of that. We must go, and go as soon as we can!'

They all went out on to the terrace to look at the weather. To the east it had cleared slightly, but the west was black and threatening.

'This break will last another two or three hours,' Monsieur Corzon estimated. 'We'd better make use of them.'

Madame Juillet, Monsieur Sala, and the Trévidic brothers

came splashing along the covered way from the houses, carrying the empty aluminium containers which had held the breakfast. Anxious faces crowded to the windows. A cluster of seniors stood at the top of the steps outside La Vallière, staring towards the headmaster's house. Everyone waited.

Monsieur Brossay beckoned to the distant Monsieur Sala. The little man handed his burden to Job Trévidic and hurried along the duckboards Monsieur Juillet had arranged between the terrace and the covered way. His face was pale and hollow under his floppy hat, but his dark eyes gleamed with pleasure. Monsieur Brossay shook his hand and said a word or two of thanks for the way in which he had behaved the night before. But this was merely a preamble. He lowered his voice.

'If you were suddenly given the choice of going or staying, which would you take?'

Monsieur Sala had sense enough to realize that this was not put to him personally as a master under notice, but as a representative of the little community.

'I'd go,' he said unhesitatingly.

'Why?'

'Last night I saw the garden flooded and that was enough to convince me of the danger we run here! The rain hasn't done with us yet.'

He spoke concisely, unhesitatingly, and this had all the more effect upon Monsieur Brossay.

'Get the boys ready,' he decided. 'See they put on their warmest clothes and carry their bedding in a roll. And no more than that! We move off in thirty minutes.'

The evacuation went like clockwork and with an almost military precision. The Trévidic brothers, working up to their waists in water, began by laying a duckboard path on trestles from the end of the covered way to Mérovée's Tower. From

the mound on which the old mill stood it was possible to jump straight on to dry ground, the left bank of the drive, and walk along it to the road without getting wet.

The three vehicles belonging to the school were drawn up by the side of the road.

'We should be able to take about twenty at a time,' was Monsieur Juillet's estimate.

The youngest were marshalled together for the first batch. They filed along the duckboards to the Tower, where Monsieur Corzon 'frisked' those whose bedding rolls looked suspiciously bulky and confiscated any excess baggage. Nonetheless little Jozas managed to smuggle his spare stock of chocolate through the customs and Kiki Dubourg his two volumes of *The Three Musketeers*.

It was hardly raining. There was just a thin drizzle which left the horizon clear above their Mount Ararat, the Arcy woods rising above the valley. They could see groups of refugees making their way there along the roads which were still above the floods.

Monsieur Boris bundled five of the youngest into the Deux Chevaux and accelerated down the empty road. His first mile and a half was clear, then came the unknown, a submerged section of the road. This, the most tricky stage of the operation, was hidden by the bend at Le Gué-d'Anjou, where a group of farms was cut off by the floods. Ten minutes passed. Their hopes were beginning to sink when the Deux Chevaux shot back round the bend. Monsieur Boris was alone at the wheel. They could get through!

Monsieur Juillet loaded the next dozen into the blue van and roared off. Then Monsieur Brossay opened the doors of his 203. Everyone immediately became very formal. Madame Brossay and Edith stood back for the boys and the boys giggled and shoved to make way for them. Father Fabien's voice thundered out and stopped that nonsense.

As she got into the car Edith turned towards the gate and waved. Charpenne was clinging to the wrought-ironwork with several others and he took the smile she gave them all as being for him alone.

Monsieur Boris had already turned the Deux Chevaux. The van with its greater clearance made the round trip in record time. In the confusion of this succession of departures, strict order was lost and the boys were picked up more or less as they stood. The wind had risen again gustily and noisily as the sky grew even darker in the west. Suddenly the mask of heroism slipped and the last to leave went in a disorderly panic.

'Hurry!' growled Monsieur Juillet. 'If the rain comes down again I won't be able to see ten yards in front of me.'

They nearly had to use force to get Father Fabien, old Monsieur Corzon and the Juillets' daughter aboard. The Deux Chevaux had not come back. The 203 and the van were loaded to the doors and a bare half-dozen refugees were left standing by the roadside.

'The van'll come back to pick you up!' Monsieur Brossay shouted and slammed the door of his car. 'There'll be plenty of room.'

'I'll be back in ten minutes,' Monsieur Juillet promised. 'We'll have enough space for extra supplies. Tell Job to look out the . . .'

The rest was lost in a gust of wind. The two vehicles sped along the gleaming road and disappeared behind the houses of Le Gué-d'Anjou. By now a thick curtain of rain whitened the far horizon.

Five minutes passed, then ten, then a quarter of an hour. It was growing darker and darker. A distant rumble rolled across the floods. It was not thunder. There had been no lightning flash to herald the mighty murmur that boomed above the waters. There was still no sign of Monsieur

Juillet's blue van at the end of that mile and a half of road which emerged from the waterlogged fields. And soon there was no road.

In the twinkling of an eye it had disappeared as though by magic. Monsieur Sala was the first to notice and he shouted to warn the others. The waters of the Loire were pouring down in a tidal wave two miles wide which fanned out in foam and a whirl of wreckage.

They shot through the gate, sprinted along the duck-boards and dived into the nearest building, La Vallière.

'Upstairs!' Monsieur Sala bellowed, chivvying and chasing the laggards.

Only when they reached the first floor did they pause for breath. Some dared to look out of the window. A muddy sea billowed down the drive, poured through the gate like a mill-race, foamed against walls and trees, shivered windows and made matchwood of doors, and flooded gurgling into buildings. Nothing could stop it as it crashed on and filled the courtyard with a deafening din.

Then the thunder of the waves grew gradually less, fell away and died in the inexhaustible murmur of the pouring rain.

Monsieur Sala had run to one of the front windows to watch the waters do their worst. At last, and only when he had seen the flood reach its peak midway between ground and first floor, did he come out on the landing and count those who remained.

There were seven, himself included.

Vignoles, pale but self-controlled, was one of them, and indeed Monsieur Sala would have been surprised not to have found him there. Picard's red face, hardly recovered from the shock of panic, showed signs of its owner's concern as to where his next meal was coming from. Charpenne's eyes were glazed, his expression sulky as he stood dreamily apart bewailing inwardly the fact that he was parted from the woman he loved. Hubert Boisson de Chazelles' beaky nose jutted out as he went from room to room whistling. Job Trévidic was there, too. In his flight he had managed to snatch up one of the bags of provisions piled on the edge of the road.

'Where's your brother?' Monsieur Sala asked him anxiously.

'Left in the van!'

Half-hidden behind the others was another boy. His goat-like face was green with fear, he cowered in a corner on the floor like a heap of rags, his body shaking with sobs. It was Chomel.

'What are *you* doing here?' Monsieur Sala exclaimed in his astonishment. 'You should have gone in the first batch.'

'No-bo-body wa-wa-wanted me!' gulped the wretched boy.

The little man sighed. 'Well, here we are together for a few days. Let's try to make the best of it.'

There was a stealthy sound below them. Someone started upstairs, paused, went down and came up again. The refugees looked at one another. No one spoke. Their hearts hammered.

Then Vignoles walked to the banisters and looked down. It was only the water lapping blackly against the foot of the staircase.

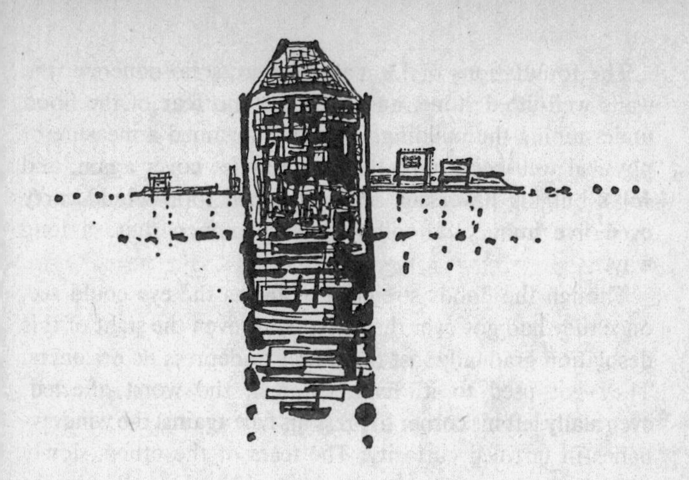

5

Vignoles, Charpenne and Boisson de Chazelles were back in their old quarters, the big room they thought they had left for good an hour before. There all of them stayed until noon, huddled together to share the warmth of their bodies. No one tried to take the lead. Vignoles's influence, however, pervaded the group, not to allocate the rations or the candles or to say who should take his turn at the continuous watch which had to be kept from the window, but to bring the others round to the shyly-framed suggestions Monsieur Sala made whenever an argument broke out among them.

All day it rained so heavily that their surroundings seemed to vanish. It was as though they were wrapped in a cloud, and in its cotton wool all their landmarks were blotted out. But the water still rose. They could gauge its implacable advance against the loop-holed wall and square windows of Mérovée's Tower. A shifting current carried isolated fragments or whole rafts of wreckage grating in sinister fashion against the walls as they swept past.

The foundations of La Vallière were solid concrete, the walls well-fitted stone, and there was no fear of the flood undermining the building. They had regained a measure of physical well-being now they were under cover again, and Job's bulging haversack with its tinned food would carry even five hungry schoolboys and two men quite a long way.

Though the floods stretched as far as the eye could see, once they had got over their first panic even the sight of this desolation gradually lost the power to depress its prisoners. They got used to it. Even Chomel, the worst affected, eventually left his corner to press his face against the window-panes in terrified curiosity. The fears of the others slowly gave ground to more material considerations. The main thing was that they were alive. Their business now was to organize things so that they should remain so for the next four or five days. All things considered, their dangerous-seeming situation was much better than that of the home-less wanderers in the gloomy undergrowth of the Arcy woods.

But Vignoles could not rid his mind of the amazing sight he had seen as, twice in twelve hours, the invading waters had swept in. All the dykes were down. Their fate now rested on the whim of the weather, a change of wind, a real break in the rain. But none had been forecast until the next day.

He could not go to the window without calling to mind the disaster of a hundred and forty years before. The authorities knew what had happened then and had taken steps to prevent it happening again, but by a fatal conjuncture of events history had repeated itself. He had only to look at Mérovée's Tower to realize that before the waters reached its slate-capped roof they would have covered the whole school and them with it.

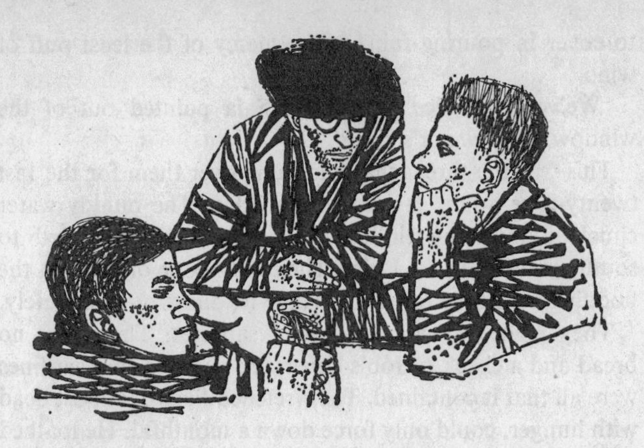

Monsieur Sala had come to the same conclusion, and he had the added load of responsibility for this handful of boys. His first steps rudely shattered the cosy inaction into which their false hopes had lulled them.

First he took Vignoles and Charpenne to one side. He lowered his voice.

'We're not going to let ourselves be drowned here. How do we know that the water won't be up to this floor by tomorrow? We must build a raft with whatever we can scrape together and be ready to escape when the moment comes.'

'That's all very well,' murmured Charpenne, 'but where do we find dry land? The Arcy woods are a couple of miles away as the crow flies and the current's bound to be stronger on that side.'

Vignoles knew the countryside like the palm of his hand.

'The floods must form a broad lake stretching to Beaufort and Longué,' he said reflectively. 'Beyond there the land rises high enough to remain above water. That's where our escape route lies. But we'll have four or five dangerous miles to cover in pouring rain, at the mercy of the least puff of wind.'

'We've no choice.' Monsieur Sala pointed out of the window. 'The water's rising.'

This was the threat that had hung over them for the last twenty-four hours. It was now midday. The muddy water chuckled under the window. The current ran from north to south, away from the Loire. Their only hope of a fall in the flooding would be for it to change its direction completely.

They made a meagre lunch of sardines. There was no bread and a check of Job's haversack revealed that sardines were all that it contained. The wretched Picard, almost dead with hunger, could only force down a mouthful. He loathed fish in any shape or form.

'I hope your "cannon-balls" keep you going the rest of the week!' the Vicomte snorted sarcastically.

For the first time that day there was a laugh.

Monsieur Sala took the opportunity to mention the raft. Apart from the two to whom he had spoken, no one had even considered undertaking such a venture. The waste of waters which covered the countryside scared them too badly. Vignoles argued that if the rafts were really solidly built the risks which they would run would be limited.

'Sooner or later,' he added, 'we shall be driven out by a real flood tide. In a matter of hours, if the rain has been as heavy in the rest of France, the water from all her tributaries will be pouring down the Loire. Nothing can stop it reaching us. We'll have to be ready!'

Chomel was the only one to rebel against the decision.

'*I'm* not shifting!' His voice was sulky and he would not look the others in the eye. '*I'm* not that crazy!'

'The first thunderclap'll make you change your mind, you silly little fool!' Charpenne retorted harshly. 'Finish your sardines and give us a hand.'

Job Trévidic was already rummaging in the attics overhead for anything that would float. Unfortunately, in view of the number of passengers and the scantiness of the material at their disposal, it soon became clear that they would have to build not one, but two rafts.

The first was finished in four hours. To a base of two wooden bed-frames a miscellaneous collection of chair seats, tins, old tubs and planks torn from the dormitory partitioning was lashed with wire and sheets plaited into ropes. They carried it downstairs to the gloomy patch of water that filled the hall. Job volunteered to test it. As soon as he stepped aboard it lurched and tipped its captain overboard. The Breton pulled himself out of his cold bath by clutching the banisters and stood, dripping wet and furious. He made a second and less energetic attempt and called to Picard and Vignoles. With three aboard her the raft floated after a fashion, provided her passengers lay on their stomachs and kept still.

They went straight on with the second. At first Boisson de Chazelles had dodged the work, but now he was co-operative and lent all the help he could. Exploring the bathrooms, his was the bright idea of unfixing the hot-water tanks. These they emptied and replugged and then used as floatation chambers on the new raft. All that was necessary was to lash a whole pitch-pine partition securely over them. When they tested it, the new raft proved the better of the two. It could carry four people with sufficient freeboard.

Every so often Monsieur Sala would leave the shipyard to glance outside. Night was falling. The second window from the bottom of the old mill was now under water. He opened the window and leaned far out over the sill. The flood-level was close now, a mere four feet from the first floor. The rain had eased, but the horizon was still blotted out and not a light flickered upon the grey and gloomy waste of waters darkening in the dusk.

Vignoles came into the room and leaned out of the window as well. He quickly pulled back.

'What are we going to do?' he asked numbly. 'If we decide at all we've got to decide now. Are we going to risk all at one throw?'

'It would be madness to launch out into the night on those two crazy wrecks!' Monsieur Sala heatedly objected. 'I'm sure you could do it alone, and so could I; but what about the others?'

'I'll put it to them,' said Vignoles, and left him.

Outside, where they were putting the finishing touches to the rafts, the noise of hammering ceased abruptly. Petrified, Monsieur Sala waited, hoping not to hear the verdict that would doom them even more speedily to their deaths.

A little later Vignoles returned, hanging his head.

'They wouldn't!' he raged. 'They called me a coward. All of them. Chomel was the first. A few hours from now will we even have time to jump out of the windows? Not one of them even looks as though he understood. They just anchor themselves to their beds, their tins of sardines and the candlelight.'

'Not one of them has your maturity, that's all,' Monsieur Sala said gently. 'You must make allowance for the fact that they're just not grown up. And you can't even pick them up and chuck them into the water!'

'What would Monsieur Brossay do if he were in our shoes?'

'No more than we've done already. Even when things were beyond his power to remedy them, he would try, to the last minute, to keep them from panicking. That's what you and I have been doing all day and we must go on doing it, one eye on them and the other on the danger that threatens us.'

Once again Vignoles leaned out of the window and looked up at Mérovée's Tower in front of him. Its massive shadow stood out against the dusk. An old loading-bay still surmounted by its pulley beam opened level with the first floor and directly opposite the dormitory windows of La Vallière. At this point there was a bare twelve feet, the width of the path leading to the kitchen garden, between the buildings.

Vignoles turned abruptly to the door.

'Are there any ladders in the loft?' he called to Job Trévidic.

'Two,' the Breton answered. 'A big one and a little one. You didn't want to use them. They're so heavy they wouldn't float.'

They were real old farm ladders, with knotty rungs and massive uprights hacked out of tough wood. The bigger was ten feet long, the smaller six.

Helped by Job and Picard, Vignoles brought them down. They were beginning to realize what his plan was as they dragged them into the dormitory. Monsieur Sala opened the main window. Outside was a narrow balcony and directly opposite and on their level the dark yawning bay giving into the tower.

Vignoles balanced the larger ladder between two beds, jumped up and down on it and ran along it on all fours to see if it would take his weight. It passed the test and so did the smaller one.

'If we can manage to lash them together securely,' he told the others, 'they'll reach the bay opposite and we can get into the mill. If we get across we'll have several days' respite and perhaps the chance of coming out alive. Well, what's your verdict?'

At once the boys dissolved in angry argument. The Vicomte and Chomel began to shout accusations at Vignoles and his friends. They would kill them all with their crazy useless plans. But Job had already made up his mind. Asking nobody's permission, he fell upon the smaller raft and tore it to pieces in order to recover the forty-odd feet of wire that had been used in its construction. The others nearly came to blows. Chomel crouched sulkily in the shadows, coiled to spring upon Job. Charpenne knocked him reeling against the banisters.

White with rage, Boisson de Chazelles sank to insulting his opponents.

'You're no friend of mine,' was his parting shot at Vignoles, 'not now, anyway!'

'I never have been,' the latter shrugged dryly. 'Try to get a little sense in your thick heads. We gave you a chance to escape, and when the moment came, you were too scared to take it. Well, now we're giving you the chance of staying alive a few hours longer and still you hesitate!'

From the gathering dusk outside came the sound of rushing water. They dashed to the window. Like a river in spate round the pile of a bridge, the flood poured round the mill, which split the current. Where it met again between the two buildings it formed turbulent whirlpools. Angry waves slapped the walls. In less than half an hour the water had risen more than three feet and was now well over half-way up the stairs.

This threat stopped their arguments at once and convinced the bitterest opponents of the plan. In the candlelight they went to work. Job Trévidic and Vignoles joined the two ladders. They overlapped the ends by a good two feet and strengthened the wire binding by tight rope lashings round the uprights. Picard was the heaviest. He tested the joint. It held firm.

It remained to lower this drawbridge and secure it in the loading bay of the mill. Job and Charpenne went up to the attic, where a mansard window was set just above that of the dormitory. With them they took a dozen sheets plaited into a rope which they lowered to the balcony. In the driving rain this was secured to the end of the ladders and then foot by foot their bridge was pushed out over the swirling waters. The slightest mistake on their part would send it crashing down, to be swept away by the current. Picard went up to the attic to help the other two, and between them they kept the rope tight and paid it out gradually, giving the necessary purchase so that the ladders slowly pushed out across the gap in a straight horizontal line. Those below slid the uprights over the edge of the balcony. Vignoles sat astride the concrete balustrade, his legs wound round the supports, leaning well out over the water to direct operations. The greater the overhang the harder it became, and the last six feet were only won inch by inch and at the cost of an effort which exhausted them.

At last the tip of the ladder brushed the wall of the mill, was gently lowered to rest on the edge of the yawning opening and lay firmly in place.

'Five minutes rest to get our breath back,' Monsieur Sala decided as he wiped the sweat from his face.

Vignoles anchored the uprights to the balcony and then went up to the attic to help the lowering party. Twenty feet of rope remained and this Job coiled and firmly knotted to the nearest beam.

While this had been going on Chomel had sat apart, gritting his teeth in rage and not lifting a finger to help them.

When all was finished he walked over to the window.

'After you, gentlemen!' he sniggered.

This was a challenge. Vignoles had guessed that something of the sort might happen and that it would fall to him to lead the way for the others. He took off his waterproof to give himself more freedom of movement, hung his torch round his neck and climbed on all fours on to the narrow bridge.

Charpenne focused his torch on him to light him on his way. They watched his progress yard by yard above the water swirling blackly round the mill.

Half-way across he turned and looked over his shoulder.

'Firm as a rock!' he called to the others.

'Don't be an ass!' Charpenne shouted back. 'Get over as quick as you can and tell us what the old rat-hole's like.'

Vignoles soon reached the opposite wall and stood upright in the loading-bay. The beam of his torch flooded the interior of the mill. He was on the second floor, which must have originally been the grain store. The worm-eaten planks creaked under his feet, there were great gaps between them where they had shrunk, and they sagged dangerously in the middle of the room. Through the holes in the floorboards he could hear the water gurgling below. Twelve feet above him was another floor supported by enormous beams. A steep wooden staircase led up to it. There was no hand-rail. Satisfied by his inspection Vignoles turned and to the horror of his friends began to make his way back along the ladder. He was determined to take personal charge of the evacuation and be the last to leave their threatened refuge in La Vallière.

When he was back on the balcony he could reassure them firmly.

'The ladders will hold. Anyone still silly enough to say they won't go?'

No one breathed a word. Not even Chomel protested.

'You go over first,' Vignoles said to Monsieur Sala. 'Picard'll follow you, so you can both be at the window to help the others in and see they go up to the floor above. Job, you'll take the supplies and I'll come last with some of the bedding rolls.'

Monsieur Sala had to take a firm grip on himself to master the fear that welled up inside him as he began his journey along the ladder, his hands clutching the uprights, his knees groping for the support of the rungs. Six feet below him the dark water seemed alive, as it slowly swirled and murmured and small whirlpools gaped and closed on its surface.

Vignoles, Charpenne and Job held their torches high to light his slow progress towards the black hole in the side of the tower. An ill-fitting overcoat which made the little man look even smaller, a floppy hat, a reputation for clumsy ineptitude, all these tended to make him a figure of fun, even at a moment as dangerous as this, but only Chomel sniggered in the background.

Monsieur Sala reached the other side safely and there was an obvious sense of pride in the way he got to his feet, his thick-lensed glasses glittering in the beams of the torches. Picard followed him without a hitch, despite his weight and the roll of bedding he insisted on carrying.

'Who's next?' Vignoles asked as he turned to the others. He did not want to rush them.

Chomel cowered behind the little group. Pride made the Vicomte step forward and fear made his legs seem to belong to somebody else; but he would have lost his honour had he hung back when the weedy little Monsieur Sala had so unhesitantly gone forward. Hubert de Chazelles got across without making a fool of himself.

'Next, please!' Vignoles's voice was insistent.

He leaned over the balustrade, the rope salvaged from the little raft coiled to hand in case anyone missed his footing or the ladder snapped in the middle. Job Trévidic shrugged the big haversack more comfortably on his back. In it was their staple diet, those wretched tinned sardines. Sensibly he stood in his stockinged feet, his heavy boots hung round his neck He was over in a flash, scuttling across on all fours like an ant, never missing a rung.

Charpenne hesitated. Vignoles looked at him and smiled. He had had a hand in the composition of the last sonnet to Edith.

'Off you go!' He lowered his voice. 'And don't forget to leave your heart in the gutter!'

Charpenne willingly took the plunge. For him the peril seemed suddenly to have decreased.

Vignoles was left alone with Chomel.

'Are you ready?'

He spoke unhurriedly and smiled, but the coward recoiled foot by foot like a wild animal at bay, warily watching Vignoles's slightest gesture.

At the other end of the bridge Picard and Monsieur Sala were getting anxious.

'Do hurry! Tell Chomel he'll be quite safe. If need be rope him to you.'

This distracted Vignoles. He heard the dormitory door slam and felt a wave of anger against Chomel's obstinacy. By deliberately disobeying orders and hesitating at the critical moment he might bring disaster by his cowardice. He was a dead weight who endangered those around whose necks he was hung. Vignoles dashed out on to the landing.

Chomel had locked himself in one of the rooms opposite. The other broke down the door with the energy of despair and found the coward concealed under a bed. He kicked him from his hiding-place.

'Don't you touch me,' Chomel growled threateningly. 'Run off to the others: I'm staying here.'

Vignoles had brought the twenty feet of plaited and firmly knotted sheets.

He showed him the coil.

'I'm going to tie one end under your armpits,' he said gently, mastering his anger. 'Monsieur Sala and Picard are waiting for you on the other side. You'll be quite safe, and we'll be able to shelter in the mill as long as we need.'

Suddenly he raised his voice to a shout.

'But if you stay here half an hour longer, Chomel, as God's my witness, I promise you'll be beyond our help.'

His appeal melted Chomel's stupid obstinacy. He allowed the rope to be bound round his chest and followed his companion to the balcony.

'Don't be scared, I've got you safe,' Vignoles encouraged him. 'Come on!'

Chomel's legs trembled as he got over the balustrade and began to crawl along the ladder. He looked down, and the nearness of the dark water terrified him more than empty air would ever have done.

It was now completely dark. The rain came down even harder and made their torch-lit rescue operations all the more complicated. A fresh wave thudded against the opposite wall of the Tower. The water between the buildings rose suddenly. The backwash reached the balcony and trickled into the dormitory.

'Go on!' Vignoles shouted as he saw Chomel hesitate and then back away.

'I can't!' the other stuttered abjectly and clutched the balustrade.

The flood swirled and swelled below the ladder and began to lap at the rungs.

One violent shove and Vignoles had pushed Chomel right out into the water, leaped on to the ladder, paid out the rope from his shoulder and made one dash across to the other side, towing the wretched boy behind him. Chomel struggled against the current, shouting pitifully.

Monsieur Sala and Picard were waiting for Vignoles on the other side, steadying themselves with one hand against the sides of the loading-bay. They caught him with welcoming arms and all three began to heave on the rope.

Chomel bobbed up to the surface, coughing and spluttering, and they hauled him in like a sack of grain.

'Do you understand now?' Vignoles shouted and shook him roughly. 'Look!'

From opposite came the sound of the flood invading the dormitory. The sudden pressure of air and water forced open the doors with a noise like gun-fire and filled the building with a groaning, a whistling and a hissing like those in the hull of a sinking ship.

Hardly knowing where he was, Chomel was pushed upstairs to the round room grey with the flour of two hundred years, in which the others were already making themselves comfortable. The ceiling was lower here, for above them were the massive rafters supporting three pairs of millstones, the wooden cog wheels and the shaft from the sails. The latter had been cut off flush with the conical roof which Monsieur Brossay had had carefully re-tiled. Two broad skylights lit the top room.

A flight of steps led upward. Vignoles drew himself through the trap-door, raised his torch and let the beam play among the tangle of beams above their heads. The pair of owls could not long have survived the last miller, but his calendar was still there, cut into the wood, whitened by age, with the point of a knife:

Today, 15 October 1820, I Jules-Henri Mérovée,
master miller . . .

The wrath of heaven had broken earlier in that bygone year. Charpenne read over his shoulder.

'A whole week!' he murmured thoughtfully. 'They lived through their flood.'

'And we'll live through ours,' said Vignoles, gritting his teeth.

They went down to the others in the flour-room. Monsieur Sala, Job Trévidic and Boisson de Chazelles were squatting cross-legged on the floor, their backs against the wall, talking peacefully together by the light of a candle stuck in the middle of the room. Chomel was in a corner, wrapped in three sets of blankets and trying to get warm again. No one had the heart to scold him. All he did was stare round-eyed with an expression of frightened obedience at Vignoles.

At seven o'clock in the evening Picard was digging into a tin of sardines with the point of his knife.

'I'm beginning to get used to these,' he said, chewing with evident pleasure. 'If anyone can't manage his share, I'll help him out.'

The loop-holes in the wall and the skylights in the roof allowed icy draughts to play upon them the whole time. They all lay down side by side, along the wall least exposed to them, close together to share the warmth of their bodies. At either end of this line of blanket-wrapped mummies lay Monsieur Sala and Vignoles.

Some were so utterly weary that they went to sleep at once. The cold, or an anxiety they could not stifle, kept the others awake much longer. For the past forty-eight hours Vignoles's nerves had been keyed to breaking-point and at midnight he was still wide awake, his eyes staring into the darkness, his ears strained to catch the slightest sound.

Could they really be above the reach of the floods here, free at last from the peril which had dogged them and had made the last few days days of torture? Cold as he was, sleep swept over him a little after midnight.

He dreamed he was back in a Château-Milon that sweltered in the sun. Evening prep was just finishing and Monsieur Juillet, dressed as a town-crier, was walking up and down under the plane trees, beating his drum. The noise awoke him.

He sat up, his brain clearing at once. Someone was knocking on the planks on which they lay, knocking repeatedly in the darkness, pathetically, insistently, wearily, like a man at the end of his endurance.

Vignoles fumbled among the blankets for his torch. He switched it on and the beam swept the walls to focus on the square hole at the top of the stairs. Through it flowed something dark, something which spread across the dusty floorboards, now creeping, now leaping forward to engulf them as they slept exhausted.

The water was on them already.

'Get up!'

Monsieur Sala, Job and Charpenne staggered sleepily to their feet. They had to shake the others, who turned and grunted, trying to regain their warmth and clutching a thread of sleep. Half a minute later they stumbled ten feet higher up among the machinery of the mill.

The draught from the two skylights shook the cobwebs. The unwearied rain pattered on the slate roof and dripped through the holes the gale had torn in it. They threw themselves down wherever they could find room between the beams, the millstones and the gigantic cog-wheels of the mill. They had not the energy to groan, let alone to complain. Those who had been lucky in where they flopped down, went back to sleep almost at once. The hopelessness of the situation that had tormented their minds had no more power over their strained and exhausted bodies.

Nonetheless somebody near Vignoles was quietly crying, his shoulders shaken by sobs he could not control – it was Chomel.

Vignoles felt his dislike melt away. What right had he to think badly of the others when all were in such a terrible predicament? Chomel was a rather stupid boy, but he was only one of thousands of victims of the flood and perhaps the two nights of peril he had spent in Château-Milon had uprooted his stupidity, selfishness and ill will. He draped a fold of his own blanket over him and huddled closer to protect him from the bitter cold.

'Don't cry!' he told him. 'The worst is over. From now on the danger will grow less. It'll all be different tomorrow and tonight will seem like a bad dream.'

'Y-you think it w-will?' Chomel gulped.

'I'm quite sure! But you've got to forget, too. Forget what you were like last week. You're a different person now.'

Chomel did not answer. The sincerity in Vignoles's voice had brought him comfort. Soon he was fast asleep and Vignoles smiled in the darkness. By expressing, through pity, an optimism he did not feel, he had recaptured a real sense of hope himself.

Nobody woke up before daybreak. At about eight o'clock it was still very dark in the old mill. Monsieur Sala, Job Trévidic and Charpenne were the first to wake, but they did not stir, if only to conserve the illusion of warmth for as long as possible and postpone the appalling return to reality until the last minute.

The rain had stopped. The rush of the water was stilled. A grey, misty light gradually filtered through the skylights and exposed the agonized attitudes in which they lay twisted. At first they merely stared silently at one another without moving, each acknowledging the other with a slight glazing of the eye.

Then Job Trévidic stirred clumsily in his blankets and groaned as he straightened his stocky frame. He stepped over those who were still asleep as he went to the nearest skylight and hoisted himself on to the sill.

For quite a while he stayed hanging half out of it, looking all around attentively and in astonishment. Inside the mill the others waited hopelessly. He suddenly pulled his head back and looked at them, his eyes glinting wildly.

'The water's going down!' he croaked.

There was a rush for the skylights.

Wherever they looked grey water spread far and wide under a misty sky, a mingling of grey with grey in which the horizon was lost. There was not a ripple or a breath of wind.

Vignoles could see two pointed gable ends in front of him. They marked the site of Le Plessis and La Vallière. Farther on the ridge of a roof and a lightning conductor showed where the headmaster's house lay and beyond that the tops of the tallest trees in the garden broke the surface of this sea of grey with their leafless boughs. He leaned still farther out.

It *was* true. Along the massive walls of the Tower the water-level had sunk in the last few hours leaving a brown streak six feet broad. He heard a call from the other sky-light.

Boisson de Chazelles saw the red canoe first. It floated along on a slight current, upside down, and straight for Mérovée's Tower.

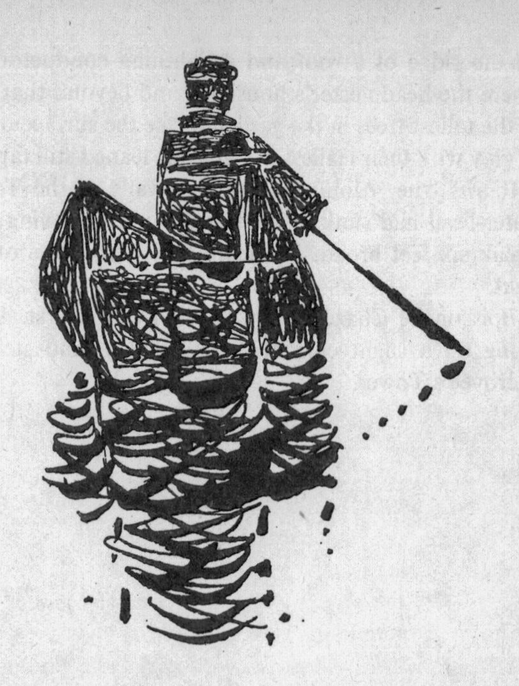

6 When it was still twenty-five yards away they realized the canoe would pass close to the left of the Tower. Monsieur Sala and the five boys made for that side. Boisson de Chazelles clambered over the sill of the skylight and let his legs hang over the edge.

'Here she comes! Pay out the rope.'

They had kept the plaited sheets which had been used to bind the smaller raft and to haul Chomel out of the water.

The Vicomte slid down and hung there just above the level of the water about six feet below the window, one foot supported by a loop at the end of the rope. A few seconds passed and then the canoe gently bumped the Tower. The force of the collision was enough to swing the red prow right round, only for the slight current to bring it back against the wall. It bumped and grated along until it was directly below the skylight.

Hubert had only to stick his other foot out to stop her. Firmly gripping the rope with one hand, he bent right down, plunged the other arm into the water, caught the edge of the gunwale and with one heave righted the flimsy craft. She danced on the water, trailing a nylon rope fixed to a ring in her stern. The Vicomte tied this to the end of his rope and very gently lowered himself on all fours into the canoe.

He gripped either side and let the boat take his full weight, to test its balance. Above him the others watched what he was doing with bated breath. When Hubert was satisfied with the results of his experiments he cast off the moorings and slowly began to manoeuvre the canoe in front of the Tower, using his hands for paddles.

For the first time one of them had broken the siege-lines of the floods and was making his escape from their prison. The self-assured way in which the Vicomte handled his little craft was miraculous. He seemed to toy with her as she skimmed scornfully over the muddy-coloured ocean around Mérovée's Tower.

'Hi! Don't go and leave us behind,' Picard called as he saw the canoe heading for the submerged school buildings.

Hubert's pride was satisfied by his demonstration and he returned obediently to his moorings under the skylight.

Monsieur Sala tried in vain to scan the distance. But the fog had clamped down upon the slumbering waters round the mill. The wind had disappeared. After four days of ceaseless bombardment by the gale the countryside lay dead and silent. Was this merely a calm before the next storm or had the elements done their worst now?

The Vicomte cupped his hands and began rapidly to bale out the water in the bottom of the canoe. Her name was painted in white on the bows – *Labrador II* – and after were the initials of the Canoe Club of France. She was a poor man's boat with her plywood hull and rather stubby lines, but she had made her long voyage safely all by herself. Any boy who was an experienced canoeist could handle her in perfect safety on such calm water, and Hubert Boisson de Chazelles was that experienced canoeist with several difficult trips to his credit. He was undismayed by whatever unknown quantity this flat grey sea represented.

He looked up at the skylight and stared Monsieur Sala in the eye.

'There's hardly any current,' he said, waving his hand around. 'I could steer straight for the Arcy woods... What do you say?'

'That's all very well,' Vignoles answered, 'but would you find them? You'll have lost all your landmarks once you're five hundred yards away from the Tower. And the fog doesn't look as though it wants to lift.'

'Oh, I know where the Arcy woods are,' Hubert assured him. This was genuine confidence, he was not boasting. 'If I keep an eye on my wake I can't miss. In under thirty minutes I'll have made contact with Monsieur Brossay, the masters and the others again. You can bet they'll be pleased to know we're still in the land of the living. Well, it's up to you to decide.'

Monsieur Sala let himself be tempted.

'Will you go on your own?'

'The canoe'll take three easily. But I'd rather have just one passenger to start with. We'll go a good bit faster and I'll have more room to steer. Now find me a couple of planks for paddles, long light ones, and I'll be happy.'

Job Trévidic hoisted himself up among the roof beams and, not bothering about adding to the damage the gale had caused, he tore down several laths. He threw the best to the Vicomte and Hubert took his pick. The first paddle strokes sent *Labrador II* skimming easily over the water.

Beneath his shapeless black hat Monsieur Sala's face was drawn as he looked questioningly at the others clustered round him. There was no doubt that the idea of appearing before Edith Brossay in all the glory of his escape thrilled Charpenne to the core. Picard and Trévidic were tough and courageous, but they feared the loneliness and the danger of the days that faced them in the Tower. There was nothing they would have liked better than to feel Mother Earth beneath their feet once more. Chomel shivered feverishly under the blanket draped poncho-wise around his shoulders. Calm though the floods now were, they still terrified him, but he would have overcome his fear to escape their cold and lonely prison. As for Vignoles, he considered it only natural that he should be the last to leave. In fact, however, not one of them dared voice his claim to the privilege of sharing in the escape with the Vicomte.

At last Monsieur Sala spoke embarrassedly.

'Settle it among yourselves.'

'If you ask me,' Vignoles suggested, 'the youngest should be the one to go. Chomel shouldn't have been here anyway. He should have left Château-Milon with the first batch. He must be Monsieur Brossay's biggest worry.'

He turned to the shivering boy.

'You'll be quite safe. The canoe's sound as a bell and old Hubert knows what he's doing. In under an hour you'll be back with your friends. There'll be people to look after you and this horror will be over.'

Nobody objected. Chomel got up without a word and they helped him through the skylight.

Below them, Boisson de Chazelles dug his fingers into the rough surface of the wall to hold *Labrador II* against the

Tower. His passenger slid down the rope, his feet touched the bottom of the canoe and at once he knelt amidships to help balance her.

Hubert squatted in the stern. Gently he pushed her off, took his lath in both hands, dug the point into the water, smoothly drew it back and headed for the open water.

Those who were left behind squeezed into the skylight to watch the canoe and its lucky crew pull away towards dry land.

'If the weather holds,' the Vicomte trumpeted, 'I'll be back! And I'll take two on the next trips. By lunchtime the

whole school'll be able to picnic in the woods! Be seeing you!'

'Careful!' Vignoles shouted to him. 'Mind the current and look out for wreckage!'

They watched the red stern of *Labrador II* gradually disappear into the fog and then all except Charpenne huddled under their blankets. He remained crouched on the sill of the skylight. Suddenly he raised his finger.

'Listen!' he said.

From somewhere at hand came the distant sound of engines. Across the water it came, now clear, now dim, and thick fog made it impossible to tell from what direction it was coming.

'Rescuers at last,' Vignoles murmured.

'And about time, too!' Trévidic growled bitterly.

'We can blame the weather, and nothing more,' was Monsieur Sala's soft answer. 'What rescue work could have been done in the last two days of dreadful storms? You can be pretty sure they did what they could, though.'

They could distinguish one engine note from the others. Soon it approached the mill. They waited. Then suddenly about five hundred yards away, right in front of them, out of the fog came a big grey launch of the River Conservancy, heading slowly downstream for Angers, its narrow deck packed with survivors.

Monsieur Sala and the others began to shout like madmen, but nobody heard them or even seemed to notice the slate roof apparently floating on the water. The boat never changed course and was quickly swallowed by the fog.

Boisson de Chazelles and Chomel saw it pass astern of them and vanish like a ghost-ship.

'That's only the start,' the Vicomte quietly remarked. 'Once this pea-souper lifts there'll be a fleet of them out between Saumur and Angers... Keep an eye on my wake, there's a good chap. We mustn't miss that confounded wood or we'll be down to the Atlantic by Paimboeuf or Saint-Nazaire in a couple of hours.'

The current thrust against the port side of the canoe, but it was as yet quite weak and *Labrador II* hardly drifted. However, the whole weight of water seemed inspired by that same steady irresistible movement although the only sign it gave was an occasional broad swirl on its surface.

When the roof of the mill had completely vanished behind them the two boys found themselves alone on the fog-bound waters, their course marked by the occasional tree-top, roof-ridge, or telephone pole with trailing wires. With no mark to guide him the Vicomte paddled by dead reckoning and kept the current full upon his port beam.

A peculiar sight showed them they had covered the first half of their voyage, for they soon saw, standing out above the muddy water, a signpost which read : *La Bohalle 2 miles – La Ménitré 3½ miles*. They were at the cross-roads on the slight rise between Château-Milon and the cluster of farms of Le Râteau.

'Well, we're on the right course,' Hubert announced calmly and lengthened his stroke. 'At the moment there can't be more than four or five foot of water under the keel. If the launch comes this way she'll have to be careful she doesn't run herself aground.'

If they leaned out they could make out the tarmac of the road between the lighter patches of the grass verge.

A little later Chomel sat up.

'I think I can see the wood,' he said. 'But we've drifted a long way.'

On their left a dark green island slowly emerged out of the fog. It was the lower wood of tall saplings crowned by pines, in whose ranks the gale had carved great gaps.

Hubert slewed the canoe round and put more pressure on

the paddle. *Labrador II* moved steadily against the current. The hill-top, which the floods had spared, stood out more clearly now with its bivouacs in the clearings and meadows, its chaotic parks of vehicles, its muddle of farm animals and here and there its shivering figures huddled round little fires. The thin columns of smoke spiralled slowly up into the calm air and there was only a shocked stillness without apparent sound or movement.

Labrador II went closer. The two boys stared ahead and tried to find in this storm-battered corner of the countryside the places they had known so well. At last Boisson de Chazelles picked out the zig-zag path which led from the woods to the lane from La Bohalle.

Thirty or so cars, all up to their axles in mud, and some on their sides, lined the slope. Chomel suddenly pointed. The blue van belonging to the school was there on the crest, almost in the undergrowth, and flanking it were Monsieur Brossay's Deux Chevaux and the Peugeot.

'I can't see a soul, but they must be there!' There was a trace of anxiety in the Vicomte's voice.

He went as near as he dared and began to follow the line of the meadow. The ebb of the water had left a broad strip of mud around the island to mark the highest level reached by the flood the night before. Not a soul was to be seen, for a fold in the ground now hid the motionless columns of smoke they had noticed a few moments before.

To negotiate a waterlogged hedgerow Hubert was forced to ease the canoe farther out. Here, too, they could clearly estimate the first drop in the flood-level from the marks on the trunks of the saplings. Then the trees grew thinner, the two boys could see the meadow once more and a motionless figure standing by the water's edge, its legs knee-deep in the muddy grass. They came closer and recognized Monsieur Brossay.

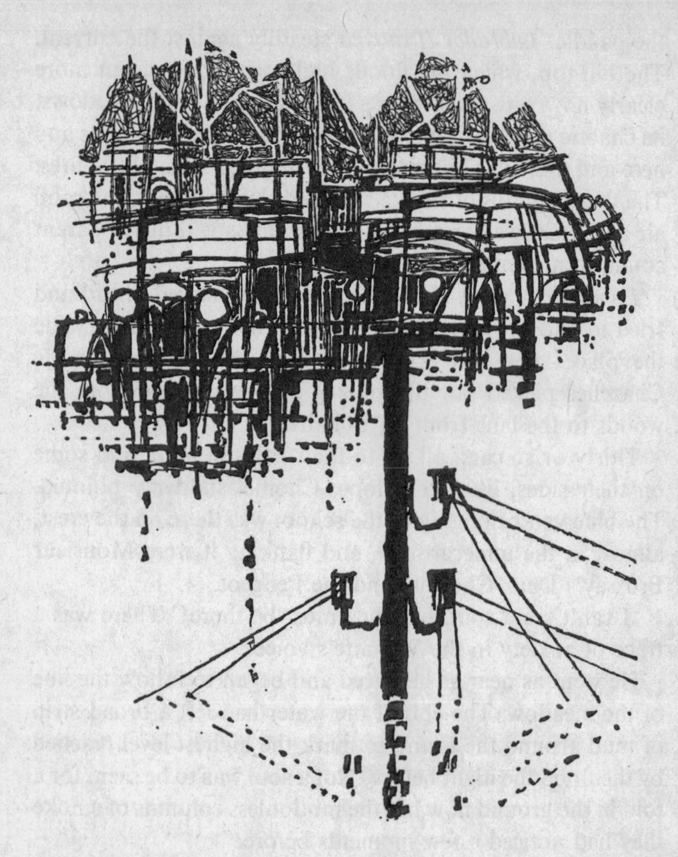

The headmaster of Château-Milon had not seen them and *Labrador II* moved too softly along the hedgerow for him to hear them either. His arms hung slackly at his sides as he faced north towards the fog-bound waters and seemed to stare at some unseen point in the shifting wall of grey.

His long brown raincoat was spattered with mud and soaked by the twenty-four-hour downpour. The rain had tangled and flattened his scanty locks around a face that was leaden and drawn with exhaustion. Something in the distance seemed to fascinate him, and his staring eyes reflected the load of fear, wretchedness and suffering which had been laid on his shoulders for the last two days.

'Ahoy there!' Chomel called and waved.

Monsieur Brossay turned sharply and saw the red canoe coming towards him with its two passengers. At first he did not recognize the boys, for the distress they had undergone had marked their features as harshly as it had his own.

Then amazement and delight chased themselves across his astonished face.

'Where have you lads sprung from?' There was a tremor in his shout.

'Château-Milon, of course!' Hubert retorted carelessly. 'Or rather what's left of it! The top of Mérovée's Tower.'

'What about the others?'

'They've stayed behind with Monsieur Sala to wait to be rescued. We'll have to get them out of there as soon as we can. The weather doesn't look as though it's going to help.'

As he told him who the others were Monsieur Brossay was making a mental roll-call. When he realized nobody was missing he began to laugh with nervous relief.

One strong stroke of his paddle and the Vicomte had grounded *Labrador II* in the grass. Chomel carefully clambered over the gunwale and stood weak-kneed on dry land.

Hubert never shifted from the stern. He was beginning to feel attached to the old canoe, and the whole business was in tune with his adventurous nature.

'We should have been finished without Monsieur Juillet,' the headmaster told them. 'I had set up our bivouac in that copse. Juillet was taking the van on his last trip when, as he was going down the hill, he suddenly saw the La Bohalle road below him vanish under water. The first and biggest wave was sweeping round the northern end of the wood at that very moment and flooding the ground that was still clear. He just had time to turn and warn us. We piled everything into the cars and the whole school got away to the lower wood a hundred yards higher up. Two minutes later the copse vanished under the tidal wave. We spent the rest of the day and all last night giving ground foot by foot as the rain, the gale and the rising floods kept us on the move the whole time. The worst sufferers from exposure have been taking turns to spend a couple of hours inside the vehicles. At least they're under cover and think they're a bit warmer. We've ten sick and a couple of injured – Monsieur Boris and Monsieur Lacour were hurt by a falling tree. Now hurry up and go back to the others. Father Fabien and Monsieur Juillet are trying to light a fire. It's worth draining the petrol tanks if it means we have the chance of a hot drink before very long.'

His tattered blanket enfolded him to the heels as Chomel made his way towards the encampment, which they could vaguely discern among the leafless trees and behind the windbreak formed by the three vehicles. The sleepers lay on the muddy ground in the twisted attitudes of corpses on a battlefield, their only protection some sheets of tarpaulin fastened to the trees. Pale, strained faces pressed against the steamy windows of the Deux Chevaux and the 203. Some way away Father Fabien, Monsieur Juillet and Yvon Trévidic moved slowly about, looking around them for what they could not find – something that would burn – and then bent to the soul-destroying task of tending a fire that obstinately refused to catch.

After a fleeting glimmer the rising sun had been unable to break through, and they were left in an indeterminate half-light that was neither dawn nor dusk. Above the fog-bank which smothered the drowned valley were doubtless more black clouds which merely needed a puff of wind to become another downpour.

The respite was so uncertain, the threat that hung over the refugees so great, that Monsieur Brossay was as torn by anxiety now as he had been during the hours of darkness or of the confusion of the storm.

'Yesterday's downpour and the sudden collapse of what was left of the embankment which followed it,' he told Boisson de Chazelles, 'must have disorganized the rescue operations in a matter of minutes. The Loire must have swept away anything afloat between Tours and Angers. All the same, as soon as there was a break in the weather, before dawn even, an old River Conservancy launch ventured out. A cockle-shell and a handful of men to rescue thousands!'

'She came by Mérovée's Tower just now,' Hubert said, 'packed with customers.'

'We aren't the worst off,' the headmaster sighed. 'Hundreds must have spent the night on their own roof-tops. The river folk on the embankment must be in an even more dangerous position. So we'll just have to wait. But how long can we last – no fire, no food, no medicines?'

The Vicomte thrust gently on the paddle to push *Labrador II* off. The red canoe slid free and bobbed on the water six feet from the bank.

'Tie her up to those bushes,' Monsieur Brossay advised him and began to walk towards the copse. 'You never know, we may find her useful during the course of the day.'

Hubert gracefully turned his craft round and struck out in the opposite direction. On the slope of the Arcy woods the only sound that could be heard was the hiss of water under the prow.

'Where are you going?' Monsieur Brossay called. His cracked voice echoed strangely in the apocalytic silence.

'To get the others!' Hubert shouted over his shoulder. 'I haven't a minute to spare. They'll be expecting me back at Mérovée's Tower in half an hour. If I'm late they'll think I've foundered.'

Monsieur Brossay stood nonplussed. Danger might strike at any moment, breaking the deceptively flat surface of the treacherous floods. The light was dim. The fog had closed in and blotted out what landmarks the water had spared.

'You're crazy!' he yelled. 'You did a first-rate job finding us in this pea-souper. Another time you may not be so lucky... Come back at once!'

Hubert screwed his head round and looked down his long nose at him without deigning to reply. The sight of the headmaster of Château-Milon standing on the water's edge, shaking his fist at him, struck him as being really rather funny, and in his confusion Monsieur Brossay used an argument which nearly split his pupil's sides.

'Come back!' he shouted at the top of his voice. 'Boisson de Chazelles, I'm ordering you to come back! If you don't turn round this very minute you can consider yourself expelled from the school!'

'What school?' the Vicomte retorted, pointing with a lordly gesture to the level flood which had overwhelmed the country round.

Ten strong strokes of his paddle took the canoe into open water, Monsieur Brossay's shouts gradually died away astern, and the fugitive was once more navigating an ocean of dank cotton wool.

He had only to keep the current on his starboard beam and to allow for the drift. Soon the Le Râteau signpost appeared to port, so all was well. Now it was merely a matter of steering north-east along the imaginary line of the flooded road.

Hubert paddled a regular stroke, but the cold was beginning to stiffen his arms. No matter, he'd done some tough canoe trips in his time and anyway it would make a wonderful story to regale his new companions in his thirteenth school, the one that would succeed Château-Milon!

'A short life but a gay one!' Hubert shouted, and raised his rate of striking.

From the skylight looking south from Mérovée's Tower Monsieur Sala and the others spotted the red patch as *Labrador II* suddenly, magically, broke through the fog. Vignoles was inwardly delighted. He had never liked the aristocratic idler. But his carelessness of any interest but his own had been a mask and Boisson de Chazelles inspired by danger was a different being.

'How did it go?' Monsieur Sala shouted.

'Not too bad! Monsieur Brossay sends his regards. But you should just see the camp – you've never seen anything so chaotic.'

He came alongside below the skylight, made fast to the hawser of knotted sheets and let both his arms drop in sheer exhaustion.

Through the opening above came a trail of smoke.

'Job found a stale bar of chocolate in one of the pockets of the haversack,' Picard explained. 'We're melting it in a pan of water. There won't be much body to it, but at least it'll be sweet and hot.'

'Well, mind you don't set the mill on fire,' the Vicomte laughed. 'That'd be the last straw. The fire brigade's got plenty of other things to do at the minute.'

The others burst into a concerted guffaw, but their laughter rang false. It hid an anxiety they could not shake off, an anxiety which matched the funereal murk of the fog on the floods and the precariousness of their refuge, which only needed a slight rise in water level to be submerged completely. Nor could they forget the horror of the night before.

Monsieur Sala leaned out and spoke to Hubert in much the same, if in milder, terms as Monsieur Brossay.

'You've done enough for the moment. Chomel is under shelter and they know we're safe. That's quite enough. I implore you not to leave the Tower. If anything happened to you I'd be the one to be blamed. So come up and have your chocolate.'

Lying flat in the canoe, the Vicomte merely shrugged. Then he glanced at his watch, sat up and faced the skylight.

'Who's coming with me? It's only just nine. Another trip'll be quite safe with three of us aboard if one of the passengers gives me a hand with the paddling. We can't miss our way. Honestly, there's even a signpost at the half-way mark!'

Monsieur Sala and Vignoles pretended to be looking in another direction and then one after the other moved away as if the problem did not concern them.

'I'm going!' Charpenne said and climbed over the sill.

Job Trévidic and Picard remained leaning in the opening, neither inclined to step forward to fill the other place. It was no good looking round the mill or outside at the fog hanging in patches of sooty black over the water.

'Make your minds up!' Hubert called, holding *Labrador II* steady against the Tower while Charpenne settled himself in the bows.

Picard, tall, strong and stolid as he was, had the build to last ten days of this draughty prison. Almost at once his courage returned. Job Trévidic, he thought, will be much more useful than I in the camp in the Arcy woods. But it went against the grain to play the Sidney Carton too obviously. He cunningly used an argument which surprised no one.

'What grub have they got?' he asked, his brow furrowed with anxiety.

'Sardines for breakfast, lunch, tea and supper!' the Vicomte replied, not that he knew, but he enjoyed pulling Picard's leg.

'Well, I'm staying!' the latter replied, his face screwed up in horror. 'There's no point in my taking this trip if there's the same menu at the end of it. Anyway, there's something about Mérovée's Tower which makes sardines taste different.'

Job made no fuss about climbing down the side of the Tower.

Monsieur Sala and Vignoles returned to lean out of the skylight and watch the others go. *Labrador II* was steadier, if lower, in the leaden water which reflected an infinity of grey fog.

Hubert cast off the moorings and pushed the canoe gently away from the wall of the mill. Charpenne knelt in the bows. His chunk of lath slid along the gunwale, and the red hull, propelled by a paddle on each beam, sped swiftly away from the Tower.

'Don't come back!' Monsieur Sala called through cupped hands. 'The water's going down the whole time and we'll be quite happy to wait here until we're rescued.'

'I'll be back in an hour!' the Vicomte bellowed back obstinately. 'You can depend on me.'

For nearly fifteen minutes now *Labrador II*'s wake had been the only ripple on the dead flat surface of the floods. Charpenne paddled easily and steadily, well able to keep the rating set by Hubert. He was a little sorry at having left Vignoles in the lurch, but he felt sure the latter would forgive him and meanwhile his romantic imagination was hard at work picturing his landing at the Arcy woods. The horrors of the night were forgotten as he calculated only the advantages to himself of the disaster and the effect his arrival would have upon Edith. How worried she must have been on his account when the seven had been separated from the others and given up for dead! Charpenne, that mixture of guile and simplicity, who harmonized his own efforts with those of Lamartine and Joachim du Bellay, felt sure that Edith would betray her feelings when she saw him loom out of the fog in the bows of the red canoe. Life was good that day, despite the dangers which surrounded them.

Job Trévidic squatted amidships, one arm gripping each gunwale, screwing his eyes to try to pierce the fog-bank. Ancestral voices whispered their warning and kept every sense tuned and alert as they sailed their sunless, boundless sea. He dipped furtive fingers in the icy water, tried to reckon distances which could not be measured, and waited the dull crunch which would capsize all three of them into this devil's cauldron. Still there was no trace of the signpost. In vain his eyes pierced the fog. All that met him was the leaden glitter where sky and dark water mingled.

Hubert Boisson de Chazelles was annoyed. Every five seconds his left arm rose in its steady stroke to bring his wrist-watch level with his eyes. The allotted interval had gone and they must have passed the Le Râteau cross-roads without noticing them. And yet the cross-current seemed no stronger than on his first trip. Where were they going? But did it matter? *Labrador II* was strong and unsinkable, her crew were no cowards and they might just as well continue their voyage into the unknown.

Charpenne was the first to get worried.

Without a word to the Vicomte he rested his paddle across the bows and the canoe swung round.

'What do you think you're doing?' the latter protested. 'Paddle on, or we'll go right off course!'

'We're in the main stream of the Loire,' Charpenne shouted. 'Look at this!'

He stuck his lath upright alongside the canoe and at once the water began to build up against its resistance. *Labrador II* lost way and then began to drift with alarming speed as though down some invisible mill-race.

'Look out ahead!' Job called.

They listened anxiously. Muffled by the fog there came the noise of thunder somewhere in front of them. Angry little waves slapped the sides of the canoe. Neither Hubert nor Charpenne knew which way to steer, for the noise seemed to come from all around them. They paused and tried to hold the rushing *Labrador*.

Suddenly less than a hundred yards ahead the line of the embankment reared up in the half-light at an angle to their course. The waters of the Loire poured across this dam in a solid sheet of which the beginning and the end were lost in the fog. Although there was the difference only of about three feet in their respective levels the spate plunged down with all its weight, the water boiling up in thunder where it fell with the noise of a cataract. Great tree trunks, huge rafts of brushwood collected here and there: forced over the embankment by the relentless pressure of the flood, they teetered on the edge for a few seconds and then fell to the other side with a terrifying crash.

The three snatched up their laths and began in a frenzy to paddle away from danger. As their headlong flight took them through La Bohalle they could see on either side the wrecked houses into which the flood had poured as through a sluice. The branches of a submerged orchard clutched at their hull and Charpenne in the bows had to paddle like a madman to avoid pieces of floating wreckage, negotiate gate-posts, shattered roofs, a line of telegraph poles or the front of a barn.

At last a broad arm of clear water opened in front of them, the current split, lost its force and then died away altogether.

Utterly exhausted, Charpenne and Job Trévidic flopped forward, arms and heads drooping. The Vicomte went on paddling *Labrador II* by himself, hoping the fog would lift or that he could find a gap in the grey wall which hemmed them in, but the half-seen sky had clouded stormily and cast its mantle of gloom over the flooded countryside.

Soon visibility was down to fifty yards. The fog drifted like smoke over the waters, now opening, now closing. For some minutes Hubert had been slowing his stroke and now he stopped paddling, not daring to venture on.

Slowly Job and Charpenne recovered in time to take Hubert's place as he in his turn collapsed, perished with weariness and cold. His air of finicky detachment had masked a human dynamo. He was one of those who had had hardly any sleep from the time the storm burst upon the school until the melancholy dawn had broken on them through the rafters of Mérovée's Tower. Before he lost consciousness he could vaguely hear Charpenne and Job arguing the toss about the points of the compass.

'I tell you it's north by there!' Trévidic waved his arms and bellowed. 'I'm a Breton and it's born in us! You head her there about or we'll find ourselves down Croisic way before we know!'

'North? There? You're off your head!' yelled Charpenne in a fury of disappointment at missing his lovers' meeting in the Arcy woods. 'You a sailor! You haven't been within miles of the sea! Listen to me, turn her and head north! Where I say it is, where it really is!'

Hubert never did find out which was the north for which his crew finally headed. Sleep pole-axed him and sealed his eyes where he knelt in the stern of the canoe. He might have been dead to the world for ten minutes or ten hours for all he knew, but the sound of voices awoke him abruptly.

The fog had not lifted, but they were now surrounded by

a setting which, breath-taking as it was, was nonetheless real. *Labrador II* floated like a gondola down a narrow street on the outskirts of Angers between two rows of houses, the windows of which were a mass of spectators. Plank bridges shakily balanced on the roofs of submerged cars spanned the intersections.

A large rubber raft with an outboard motor and a steel-helmeted crew took *Labrador II* in tow and cleft a way for the canoe through the motley collection of small boats. As they passed some squat Army landing-craft they could see the drawn, dumb looks of the homeless they had rescued. Then in front of them reared the front of a huge building to which all seemed to be heading.

'The Préfecture!' Job murmured.

The rubber raft and the canoe bumped alongside the head of a magnificent flight of steps and they could see into a gloomy entrance hall damp-stained by the flood.

In a vast room on the first floor (from its gilded ceiling and its frescoed walls it must have been the place where all the official receptions were held) some fifty people were gathered in small groups around several map-strewn tables. Gold braid rubbed shoulders with oilskins, crumpled suits and muddy overalls. There was a low hum of conversation, a fever of activity controlled by the overriding need to act quickly, decisively and economically. Telephone cables snaked across the floor from portable switchboards: from a corner came the frenzied buzz of a morse tapper. It all provided the background of noise against which the shouted orders rang with sudden and tragic intensity. There was a continuous bustle of messengers hurrying from one group to the other, dashing out of the doors like the wind and down the flight of steps, their gumboots squelching.

A police superintendent marshalled Job, Charpenne and

Boisson de Chazelles towards a table in the middle of the room. On their way the Vicomte noticed an elderly man standing to one side. His face was powerful and he was the focus of a hum of deferential activity. He seemed in charge of this power-house, feeding instructions to a closely-knit organization – the Civil Defence Forces, mobilized as soon as calamity had threatened.

He was talking to two members of the Government who had hurried there during the night.

'We were beaten!' the Prefect was saying wearily. 'And yet a few hours before the storm burst on us we had been warned and had everything ready in accordance with the Orsec Plan which controls the rescue services in the event of a national disaster. But even if our resources had been a hundred times greater we still should not have been able to curb the extent of the calamity which has struck this unlucky area. Nature has weapons which are beyond our scope and against which our weak defences are useless. All we can do now is rescue the homeless, treat the injured and feed the whole Department. For the next twenty-four hours ten or fifteen thousand lives will still be at the mercy of a whim of the weather, an unexpected rise or fall of the flood waters. If they go down too fast their destructive flow can be just as dangerous to the islands still above water...'

They made way for the crew of *Labrador II*. A whole table was covered with large-scale military maps pinned edge to edge. As the messages came in, two Air Force officers, their eyes red from lack of sleep, leaned forward to chalk a red circle round the given spot, write a figure beside it, copy the name of the place on to sheets of paper with the approximate number of the homeless there, and pass all this information to the secretary beside them, completing it by giving the map reference.

'These lads have come from the thick of it,' the superintendent told them, 'from the area we know least about, Beaufort-Longué – La Ménitré – La Bohalle.'

One of the officers looked up at Boisson de Chazelles, who now seemed the least sleepy of the three.

'Now I'm asking you to tell us what you know, not what you think,' he said gravely. 'Any mistake on your part can lead to waste and misdirection of effort. For whatever we do we must do it very quickly. Apart from the dangers already faced by those who are cut off, we have to remember what time of year it is. We are now in December and the slightest fall in temperature could be fatal. These people have no shelter, they have been soaked to the skin for the last three days. One cold night could kill thousands... Now, what can you tell me?'

Hubert thought for a moment.

'I could only see the north slope of the Arcy woods distinctly,' he said. 'I counted the fires, the parked cars and the makeshift tents on the hillside, and I should think at least a thousand people must have collected there. But there must be even more on the southern slope, all the river dwellers who must have made a mass escape from the embankment yesterday morning.'

The officer encircled the Arcy woods with a chalk line that brushed contour 22, the present flood-level. He paused before adding the round number Hubert had given him and put a question mark after it.

'Anything else?'

'Three of our friends are stuck on top of Mérovée's Tower, with the water below and the sky above. We spent the night with them and they're the ones in the greatest danger.'

'Where is this tower?'

Hubert himself took the chinograph, stuck his long nose over the map and spotted the site of the mill straight away.

He drew a heavy red circle round it. Then he stood up with an odd smile on his face. It had been a negligible gesture and yet it had in some way atoned for the waste and chaos of his life until now.

At the other end of the room one of the telephonists leaped from his switchboard, his face alight.

'The fog is lifting between Laval and Châteaubriant!' he called, pausing between each word. 'Wind, light nor-nor-easterly. The weather will clear in half an hour!'

7 Muffled in his blanket, his hat pulled down over his eyes, Monsieur Sala leaned his elbows on the sill of the southern skylight. He glanced at his watch and then stared into the distance – ten past ten and still no sign of *Labrador II.* He slid to the floor, where Picard and Vignoles bent double as they tended a tiny fire lit on a broken piece of the idle millstone.

'Monsieur Brossay must have kept Boisson de Chazelles at the camp,' he said contentedly. 'That's really the best thing he could have done...'

Vignoles looked up and began to laugh.

'You don't know our Vicomte. He just doesn't like being fenced in. He has a phobia about it. Can't be in a place for five minutes without wanting to break out. You can bet that if he's made the Arcy woods he's landed a healthy distance from Monsieur Brossay and the camp. Why, for two pins he'd throw his passengers overboard if it meant he'd get away.'

'He came to Château-Milon the same day as I did, October 3,' Picard went on. 'He hadn't been here a couple of hours before he knew all the side-doors in the school, the one by the chapel, the other by the kitchen garden and the garden gate. He'd bribed the Juillet's daughter to have her old bicycle ready for him between midnight and six in the morning. Four times he found Monsieur Brossay waiting for him at the foot of the garden wall, and then it was about turn and eight hours' detention! A month later he was still determined to get away and this time for good and all. He could hardly keep it to himself. School didn't suit his book at all. From then on it was one long game of hide-and-seek which gave the head a good few sleepless nights. Hubert wanted to run away and Monsieur Brossay wanted him to stay. So he made it his business, without appearing to, to stop him doing something which he would have to punish by expulsion. You can imagine the floods were just what the Vicomte needed!'

All three chuckled. Monsieur Sala's eyes widened and twinkled behind his thick glasses. He was delighted to be let into the secrets of the school and to discover what went on in the minds of the older boys, who made up a miniature world and were as lively, as individual and as varied as the inhabitants of a large town.

'Shall we open a tin?' Vignoles suggested, mindful of Picard's heroic fast.

'How many have we got left?' the glutton of Château-Milon asked anxiously.

'A couple of dozen.'

Picard at once divided by months and days.

'Okay,' he sighed and reached for the rucksack.

There were six sardines to the tin. Picard was given the two biggest and all the oil – they had to keep his spirits up somehow. Vignoles and Monsieur Sala amicably split the remainder between themselves. Holding the fish delicately between the thumb and forefinger, they nibbled it slowly.

When they had finished their minute meal they carefully licked their lips and fingers, sighing contentedly as though it had been an eight-course banquet. Monsieur Sala's face was covered by a good quarter inch of beard and with his wreck of a hat on his head he looked a complete tramp.

'Anyone'd spare you a copper!' said Vignoles jokingly. 'But I don't suppose Picard or I look much better. I begin to wonder if I'm not lousy already.'

By eleven the fog was as dense as ever and there was still no sign of the red canoe. In their isolation conversation gradually languished and then finally ceased.

After a while Picard broke the silence.

'If Hubert hasn't come back it means something's happened to him.' His voice was strained. 'He may be a bit of a bounder, but he keeps his word.'

'He's all right,' Vignoles retorted convincingly. 'The fact that he hasn't come back means the weather's going to clear and they're coming to rescue us in style this afternoon. You'll see . . .'

Monsieur Sala remained silent. He stroked his beard with satisfaction, cast an inquiring eye at the gloom outside, and returned to his studious thoughts, thoughts which visibly turned towards sleep.

Vignoles also looked out from time to time. He sat up with a jolt, thinking he had slept for hours instead of for the seconds his eyes had been closed in momentary exhaustion.

He was the first to realize that the weather outside was changing. It was still as gloomy, but the atmosphere within the mill seemed suddenly milder, as though the rounded walls preserved forgotten stores of sunlight, the warmth of summers long ago. He lay and waited, thinking his tired eyes had

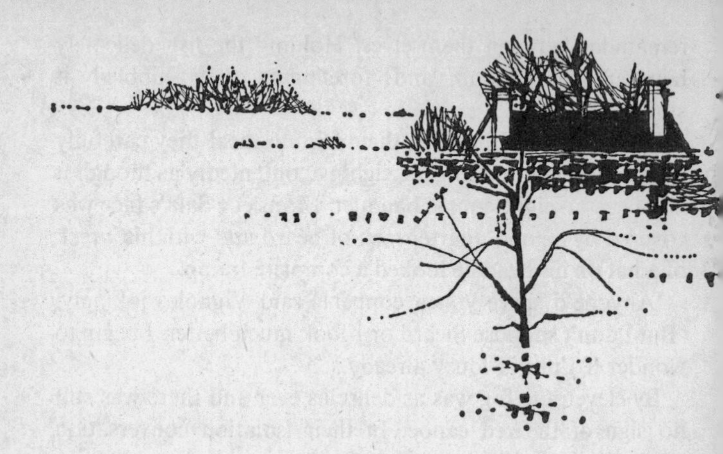

created a mirage. The gaping holes in the tiles still showed the fog, but it was definitely lighter inside the mill.

The other two woke as he shouted and dashed to where he stood at the skylight. All around the fog was lifting. As veil after radiant veil melted away, the distant heath appeared like the backcloth in some theatre as the curtain rises slowly and solemnly. To the north, beyond the roofs of the submerged school, was the blue of the countryside, with its scattering of white houses, islands of woodland and ribbons of roads and hedges that had been spared by the flood. Still farther off, beyond this earthly paradise, a broad beam of sunlight cut a golden swathe from east to west, restored at long last the horizon, and pushed back the cloud-bank from a corner of sky of gem-like, flawless, icy blue.

Neither Monsieur Sala nor the two boys could speak for sheer relief as they gazed at the miracle and watched, half-hypnotized, as the patch of blue grew ever larger and shed a heavenly sunlight which in their darkest hour they had thought was for ever extinguished. A few moments later the fog-bank above the mill began to melt and they could see the

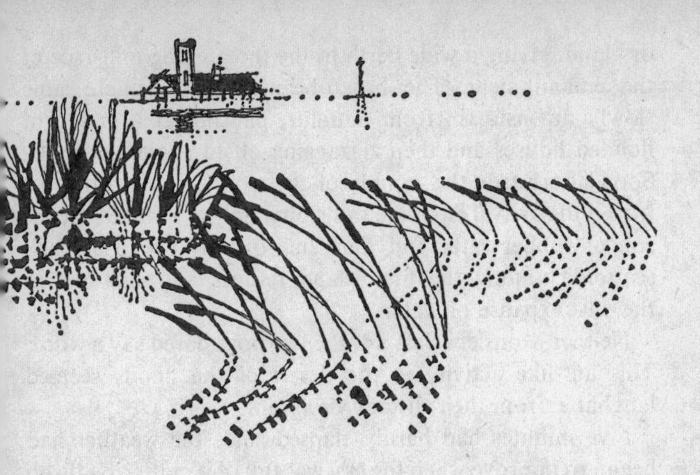

drowned countryside around them. It was like one huge lake fringed by a slender ring of dry land, with gaps here and there which seemed to lead to oceans beyond.

They hurried to the other skylight.

To the south an odd trick of the atmosphere magnified, across the waters, the pine-tufted hump of the Arcy woods. The naked eye could pick out the motley cluster of tents, the parked cars huddled at the foot of the slope and the smoke of the camp fires, blue in the fresher air.

In the background a line of foam stretched from one end of the horizon to the other, marking the submerged embankment. Beyond it the Loire in full flood raced in a tumult of waves which, despite the sunlight, kept the very colour of the catastrophe, the thick, dark yellow of the earth the waters had swept away in their journey to the sea.

'No sign of *Labrador*,' Vignoles muttered as he screwed up his eyes. 'You should be able to spot her at once in light like this.'

The improvement in the weather had lured a number of overloaded vessels from their moorings, and they headed for dry land, giving a wide berth to the threatening mill-race of the embankment. The broad-beamed grey launch came slowly downstream from Saumur, pausing at a group of flooded houses and then zigzagging off to avoid the roofs. Soon afterwards the rumble of their outboard motors betrayed the arrival from the same direction of a whole squadron of rubber rafts. But their line quickly broke as each scattered among the first island refuges and was lost in the vast expanse of water.

Neither Monsieur Sala nor the two boys dared say a word. This ant-like activity in the desert of the floods seemed laughable from their distant viewpoint.

Five minutes had hardly elapsed since the weather had begun to improve when the sky was full of a muttering throb which grew louder as the seconds passed. Vignoles looked up. The glare dazzled him and he could see nothing from the south. At that very moment Picard crossed the floor in three strides. They had not even time to ask what was happening. A shrill whistle enfolded Mérovée's Tower and almost lifted the slates off the roof, while at the same time a vast whirling shadow swept across the water close to the boys.

'An Alouette!' Picard bellowed, waving frantically. 'Two fellows in the cabin! They saw us!'

But the helicopter was now far away, speeding for the Arcy woods like some great dragonfly. Two others went right over the mill one after the other. They were so low that the downdraught of their rotors blew through the skylights. Picard climbed up into the opening, shouting and waving like a lunatic.

But they were only the forerunners of a cloud of machines which came on, wave after wave, from every point of the compass. Glittering in the sunlight, circling to pick up their objectives, breaking away to make their approach, they sank as light as thistledown to water level. The heavens had opened to bring them help!

'Make room for me!' Monsieur Sala begged as he pushed his way to the skylight between the two boys. 'I don't want to miss this!'

'We nearly missed it, anyway!' Vignoles laughed. 'And now we've got ringside seats.'

In the fantastic whirligig helicopters of all types mingled from huge Sikorskys to minute Djinns, from Vertol 'bananas' to tiny Albany air O/Ps which seemed to hang as from a thread. All appeared as chaotic as a swarm of bees, as Bells, equipped with floats, landed near a roof-top, a hillock, a piece of floating wreckage, hovered a moment on the floods, then shot up and away.

Soon there was a two-way stream of traffic above the flooded countryside. The helicopters appeared from their distant bases, performed their duties as though they were child's play, and then made off in one of three directions which must lead to the reception centres. The Arcy woods, the riverside villages of La Ménitré and La Bohalle, the cluster of farms at Le Gué-d'Anjou, the populous parish of Ilettes, seemed to draw the main formations, circling slowly before peeling off one by one in a gentle glide, to disappear into the glare reflected from the water, and then to take off once more and join the queue disappearing beyond the horizon.

Monsieur Sala and his companions had their eyes riveted to the glades of the Arcy woods. Vertol 'bananas' with their double rotors, Sikorskys, Sycamores with glittering cabins, all converged upon the low-lying meadows which provided a suitable landing-place to the west. Far away as they were they could make out the files of figures shuffling along the slopes to join the compact mass waiting by the strip. There was nothing panicky about this orderly evacuation. The big helicopters circled and landed one by one, took on their passengers, rose straight into the air with a scream of rotors and set a direct course for Angers in an unbroken aerial bridge.

'The school's sure to be ready and waiting,' Picard said enviously. 'Hope they don't forget us!'

He began to jump up and down at the skylight, waving a blanket like a flag. Every now and then a helicopter would practically graze the roof of the mill and swirl away across the floods, its rotors whirling dizzily.

Monsieur Sala looked at his watch. Midday so soon!

Rescue operations proceeded uninterruptedly around them. Sometimes a tiny helicopter, a Bell or a Djinn, would head for some minute and lonely spot. Then suddenly the ladder and life-line would come snaking out from under the cockpit.

Vignoles was growing anxious.

'Our bus doesn't seem to be running. Do you think they can see the roof of the mill? Here we are, miles from anywhere, half-way between the embankment and dry land. We'd better do something about attracting attention.'

As he looked round, Monsieur Sala noticed three sardine tins lying in a corner. He picked one up. The bottom of the tin could in the last resort be used as a mirror. Vignoles and Picard understood immediately. Only the southern skylight was in the sun, so all three of them took post there and for a minute or two practised concentrating the reflections on the water. Such a signal should be spotted even at long range. Meanwhile they watched from both sides as they waited for the first helicopter to come their way.

'Alouette on patrol above Longué,' Picard called from the northern skylight. 'She's coming this way! Stand by!'

Suddenly the whistle of rotors approached them. Picard

had already hurled himself over to the two others. The low-flying helicopter passed within five hundred yards of them on its way to the Arcy woods. They had time to aim at the cockpit cover, which flashed several times from the winking reflections of their makeshift mirrors. But the Alouette never altered course, gained height and vanished behind the clump of trees.

'She came in at the wrong angle to the mill,' Vignoles remarked. 'Let's leave the northern skylight. We've got to dazzle it right in the pilot's eyes.'

They tried five times more, seemingly with the same lack of success. The helicopters continued unwavering on their way like great, busy bumble-bees.

The sun was beginning to go down. Slowly the clouds banked up in the west, a shadowy mass across the horizon. At last, at about four o'clock, the flicker of the mirrors caught the perspex nose of a Sycamore. The giant dragonfly altered course sharply and swung close to the mill. The three survivors waved sheets and blankets wildly through the skylight.

To their intense disappointment the helicopter climbed almost at once and rapidly sheered off. But the pilot must have reported their position, for ten minutes later an Alouette appeared on the horizon from the direction of Angers and came in fast on the mill.

'This time they really have come for us!' Picard bellowed as he heaved himself on to the sill of the skylight.

In a few seconds the helicopter was overhead. Through the rounded canopy the pilot made a hand signal which perplexed them. What on earth did a single 'thumbs-up' mean?

'One at a time?' Vignoles suggested. 'I suppose he doesn't want to take any risks. Well, don't knock me down in the rush!'

The pilot steadied the Alouette at sixty feet, and then began very gently to lose height until he was right over the skylight. The downdraught from the rotor harried the three huddled in the opening. A panel on the port side of the cockpit slid open, a white nylon ladder came snaking down and after it the life-line with harness attached. Picard caught them in mid-air. What with the noise of the engine and the whine of the rotor blades they could no longer hear themselves speak. The helicopter came even lower. Picard hesitated a second and turned to the others.

'Go on up!' Vignoles yelled. 'No time for "after you"! And don't forget to send the taxi back for us!'

Picard fastened the harness and gripped the dangling ladder. A slight swing carried him away from the wall. The helicopter climbed very gently, the pilot leaning out to watch his passenger clumsily stumbling up the rungs. From below two pairs of anxious eyes watched until Picard eventually came level with the cockpit and disappeared inside.

The Alouette banked steeply, gained height and disappeared towards Angers.

'In maybe less than ten minutes it will be our turn.' There was real authority in Monsieur Sala's voice. 'And I shall be the last to leave. Is that clear?'

Vignoles smiled and nodded.

Then they leaned out of the skylight to savour at their ease the fantastic dance of the helicopters which grew ever more active as dusk set in. One had to have survived those tragic hours in the face of disaster to really appreciate the full significance of the sight, the nobility that was behind this winged army. Monsieur Sala was quite bewildered. Kant now seemed an old driveller and his *Critique of Pure Reason* a mass of nonsense. 'Good gracious, that's right. My thesis is a monumental blunder!' the little man thought frankly to himself. 'There's plenty of other things for a keen observant

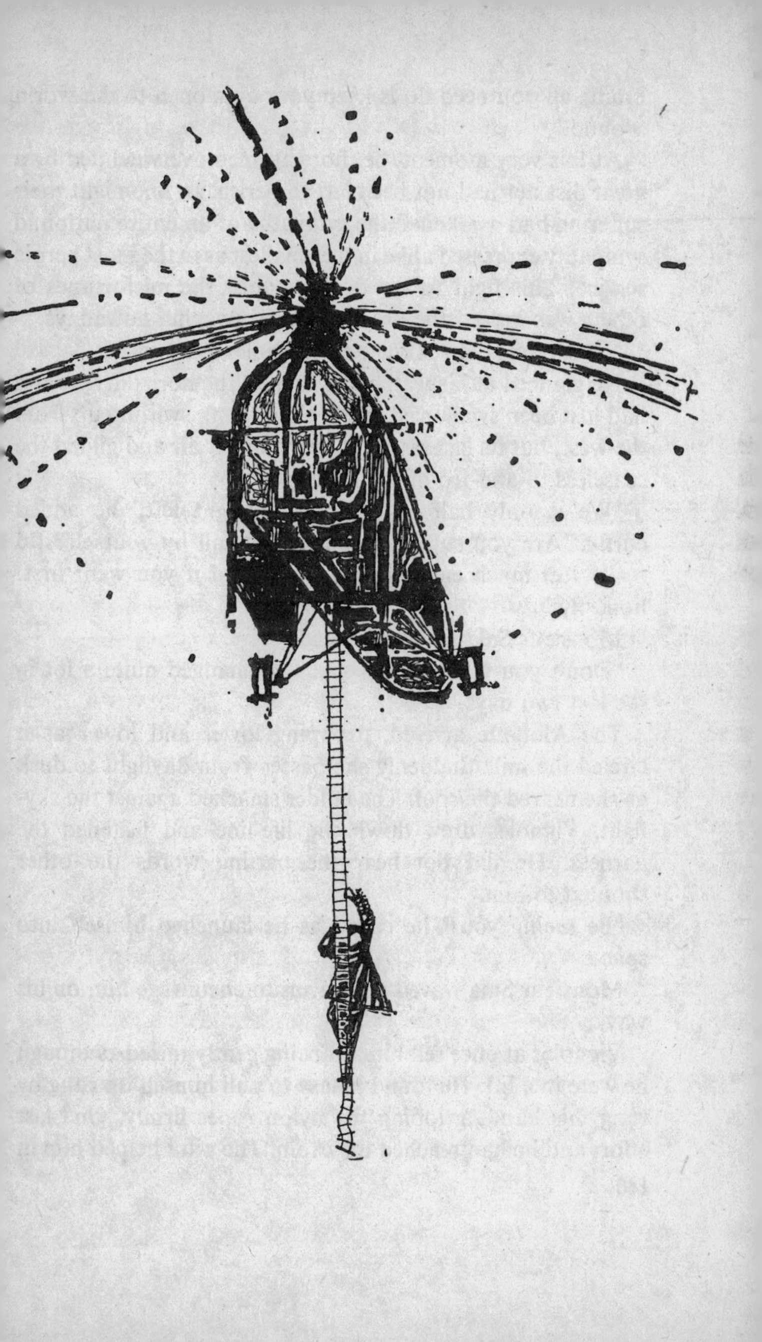

brain: all you need do is keep your eyes open to the world around.'

At this very moment, he thought, men overwhelmed by a great disaster had not been left to perish. In one night their suffering had awakened the sympathy of an entire nation, a sympathy expressed alike in the smallest as in the most heroic service. This fight to the death against the misfortunes of others was indeed the only war worth waging nowadays.

'Here comes our Alouette!' Vignoles announced.

He glanced at his watch and then at the horizon. The sun had just been swallowed in the cloud-bank swirling up from the west, but its last rays still lit the upper air and gilded the ceaseless to-and-fro of the helicopters.

'We've only half an hour of daylight left,' he added curtly. 'Are you sure you can manage all by yourself? I'd really feel much easier in my own mind if you went first, honestly.'

Monsieur Sala shook his head.

'Don't you worry about me. I've changed quite a lot in the last two days.'

The Alouette arrived, dropping lower and lower as it circled the mill. Suddenly she passed from daylight to dusk as she neared the roof. The ladder smacked against the sky-light. Vignoles drew down the life-line and fastened the harness. He did not hear the parting words the other shouted to him.

'Be seeing you!' he called as he launched himself into space.

Monsieur Sala waved both arms to encourage him on his way.

Vignoles at once felt himself being gently raised as though he were in a lift. He found it easy to pull himself up rung by rung, his hands gripping the nylon ropes firmly. One last effort and he had reached the cabin. The pilot helped him in and signed to him to haul up the ladder and close the panel. Vignoles flopped into the seat beside him.

The cockpit was cramped and although the rotor blades were out of sight their whirling made the machine vibrate. Vignoles looked out over the side and saw below them the whole flooded countryside slip giddily past, islands of floating wreckage and waterlogged ruins standing out above the surface and the idle shifting current. He turned his head and winked as the young sergeant pilot gave him a friendly grin.

'You did all right! Piece of cake at your age... Like a P.T. lesson.'

They had to shout to make themselves heard.

'If we hadn't signalled,' Vignoles yelled, 'you'd never have spotted the mill!'

The pilot's answer took his breath away and epitomized the efficiency of the Civil Defence as a whole and the good use to which each single scrap of information was put.

'No!' the pilot laughed. '*We had your address*... May've been late, but you've got to take your turn. Been sick or wounded ... had you out long ago... Take the other one off in ten minutes... Here we are!'

The daylight was dying fast. The darkening town, with here and there a light already shining, rose up to meet them, streets and flooded squares reflecting the twilit sky. The Alouette brushed the last roof-tops of the northern suburbs and came in to land beside a recently arrived Sikorsky on the strip at Avrillé, the end of the aerial bridge.

Since morning the little airfield had been the focus of an intensive two-way flow of traffic. In the first place there had been the ceaseless shuttle of helicopters to and from the floods and then there had been the taxi service to Laval of lorry, bus and private carloads of homeless.

Vignoles jumped lightly down from the cabin, his ears still buzzing.

The pilot held out his hand to him.

'I'm going back right away. My last trip. Here, take this card and mind you don't lose it. It's got your special number on it and it'll help you get back to the rest of your school. Good luck.'

The boy ducked automatically as he passed under the rotor blades. He followed the passengers of the Sikorsky as they filed in silence into one of the flying club's hangars that had been turned into a reception centre. The card the pilot had given him bore the number P72 and enabled Vignoles to pass a dozen checks, guided him through the crowd, piloted him from one official to the next, and landed him on the roadside next to a luxury coach. Its engine was ticking over and Picard's broad red face was peering out of a window.

'Hurry up! I've kept a seat for you!'

'Where are we going?' asked a rather bewildered Vignoles.

'Château-Gontier. The whole school's there.'

It was getting very dark by now. On the other side of the airfield fence the Alouette gently lifted from the ground and then leaped skywards.

'Let's wait for Sala!' Vignoles called.

'Can't! The coach'll go any moment now. Sala can take the next one. They run every ten minutes. Get in!'

Monsieur Brossay was pacing up and down outside the town hall at Château-Gontier. With him was a group of officials who were awaiting the Angers-l'Orsec coaches with equal impatience. He was still anxious, but gradually the strain was dissolving in a warm tide of satisfaction. He had safely shepherded his flock through gale, storm and flood. And yet, twelve hours before, in the tragic light of dawn, he had set a cross in his notebook beside the names of the seven who had been lost without hope to the floods. With daylight came the miracle. The first survivor – admittedly the least prepossessing of his pupils – had reached him with a temperature in the hundreds, guided over the floods by a professional escaper who had made haste to be on his way once more after broadcasting his good news.

In the early afternoon, as he stepped with fifteen of his pupils from the Vertol which had rescued them from the Arcy woods, there waiting on the airfield at Avrillé were three more, among them the aforesaid Boisson de Chazelles. Monsieur Brossay had to take a firm grip on himself to refrain from clasping to his bosom those three drowned rats, grey with cold, hunger and fatigue. That made four. There were three still missing, but their return could not be long delayed, and the headmaster of Château-Milon was mentally savouring the phrases that would grace his triumphal announcement. He would have to have a hundred copies duplicated: fifty for the parents, fifty for the local Press: '*In the ordeal through which the school has passed ... The cool courage of the pupils ... The presence of mind and the devotion to duty of the staff ... etc... etc.*' Paris had already taken as its device *Fluctuat nec mergitur*, so he had to scrap that idea. Anyway, it might have been a trifle inappropriate to apply it to buildings which had been under twenty feet of muddy water.

It was pitch dark when the coach drew in with a stream of traffic from the south. Monsieur Brossay at once spotted the burly red-faced figure of Picard through the window and next to him the thoughtful eyes and fair hair of Vignoles. Another two, and the best of the bunch. 'We'd have had it but for Vignoles and Monsieur Sala,' the Vicomte had said to him only a few minutes before. But where was Sala?

He hurried to the door to welcome the newcomers. Both bore their ordeal remarkably well despite their exhausted appearance.

'Hurry up, boys!' he called. 'The others are waiting for you. They've put us in a new wing of the local school for the night. We'll all be mucking in for our evening meal and I'm afraid you'll just have camp beds to sleep on tonight. But it won't be for long. You'll be going home to your families tomorrow.'

'What family?' Vignoles thought sadly. He had no one to whom he could recount his adventures.

Monsieur Brossay stood on tiptoe to peer into the coach, which was slowly emptying of its load of unfortunates.

'Monsieur Sala isn't with you?' he suddenly demanded. His voice had changed.

'I left him in the mill,' Vignoles answered. 'He was determined to stay to the bitter end. Our Alouette could only take us off one at a time for safety reasons. Before we left Avrillé I saw it take off and head for Château-Milon. Monsieur Sala will be here in a few minutes' time on the next coach.'

'Good. I'll wait a little longer,' Monsieur Brossay decided. His face regained the strained expression it had worn all day. 'You go on ahead. The school's down the first turning on the left. I expect you'll see Monsieur Simon or Monsieur Juillet at the gate. I'll be with you in a few minutes, then.'

When they had gone a little way Picard hastened to point out to his companion the strange contradiction which underlay Monsieur Brossay's concern.

'I can't understand the Head, really I can't. He was just waiting for the chance to give Monsieur Sala the sack, and on Saturday night he got it and that was that. But now you'd think the little man was the apple of his eye... Well, we'll see he gets him back.'

'We're all the same,' Vignoles replied. 'A couple of days ago I couldn't have cared less about Chomel, and yet when we had to get out of La Vallière in a hurry I was more worried about saving the idiot's life than I was about my own. Still, it's not worth trying to work the reasons out.'

Château-Milon had re-formed in a pleasant little school building surrounded by a vast asphalt playground ringed by flower beds. Two classrooms and a pair of studies were filled by a diabolical din as all awaited the evening meal. The sick – Chomel among them – were already in bed in the upstairs rooms, which had been turned into dormitories.

A storm of applause greeted the appearance of Picard and Vignoles. Sure in his own mind that they would emerge safe and sound, Hubert Boisson de Chazelles had enjoyably spent all the afternoon in condemning them to a lingering death. As he remarked, you needed some first-class suspense.

Questions were hurled at them.

'I'm too tired to hold a Press conference,' Vignoles laughed. 'I'll get Madame Brossay to type a few copies of my statement and I'll give them away free to anyone who wants them.'

The juniors were furious to have been taken off from the Arcy woods by anything so conventional as a dull old Sikorsky or Vertol flying omnibus. They secretly envied the escape of the two seniors on the end of a rope ladder.

Kiki Dubourg had managed to salvage the last volume of *The Three Musketeers* and the room reverberated to the thunder of Cardinal Richelieu. But Jozas was short of chocolate: his reserve supply had been washed away during the night.

That hero of the morning, Charpenne, had by evening become merely the melancholy bard racking his brains for rhymes to enrich a seventh sonnet. Edith had not even looked at him when she climbed out of the Sycamore which had snatched her from the floods.

Picard was soon his old self as he found his way through a

maze of passages to the kitchen. He came back with a face as long as his boots – the locality had just received a consignment of fresh herrings!

'And to think we left a good twenty tins of sardines in the top of Mérovée's Tower!'

'Monsieur Sala won't forget them,' Vignoles told him.

'He won't be doing badly if he comes away with those glasses of his and that old black hat!'

Monsieur Brossay did not return.

A little later a gust of wind buffeted the windows and reminded the more impressionable of the warning they had had on Saturday night. Then the rain poured down in torrents.

At eight o'clock Jeantet marched down the corridor ringing a bell. Its tinny notes could not compare with Cunégonde's golden voice, but at least tradition had been preserved.

They had their meal at little tables in a pretty dining-hall with nursery paintings on the wall. All the masters were there, including Father Fabien, whose gruff good humour was infectious. Monsieur Juillet's family and the Trévidic brothers waited on them and not even the change of scene could upset their old routine.

Madame Brossay and her daughter were at the top table, at which two places remained empty until half-way through the meal. Then, at last, the headmaster of Château-Milon came in. But he was alone, his face was gloomy, and his lips sealed the bad news which he refused to tell his neighbours.

Vignoles was one of the first to hear it, in the classroom to which the staff withdrew to confer after dinner.

'Monsieur Sala hasn't come,' Monsieur Brossay told him wearily. 'The authorities in l'Orsec know nothing about him. It was still light enough when the pilot of your Alouette reappeared over the mill. But there wasn't a soul at the skylights and the tower seemed quite deserted. He circled just above the water for at least five minutes and then flew straight back to Avrillé. He thought that one of the other helicopters on patrol had picked up Sala and taken him back to another airfield. The Civil Defence people rang round at once, but it was no good. There was no record of a rescue being made at that time and in that place. Night and bad weather have stopped all further search . . . so there we are!'

Monsieur Brossay was obviously upset. An hour before, all had seemed to indicate that the school had come through the dreadful disaster unharmed, and now right at the eleventh hour its lowliest and least appreciated member had failed to answer his name.

'Did you notice anything odd in Monsieur Sala's behaviour last night or this morning?' he asked embarrassedly.

Vignoles nearly lost his temper at this.

'If anyone kept his head in the last twenty-four hours, it was him! I don't know what's happened to him since I left, but whatever it is you can be sure of one thing: Monsieur Sala would think of the school first and himself second.'

Father Fabien's deep voice boomed from the other end of the room.

'You mustn't abandon hope for the little man. We'll find him again.'

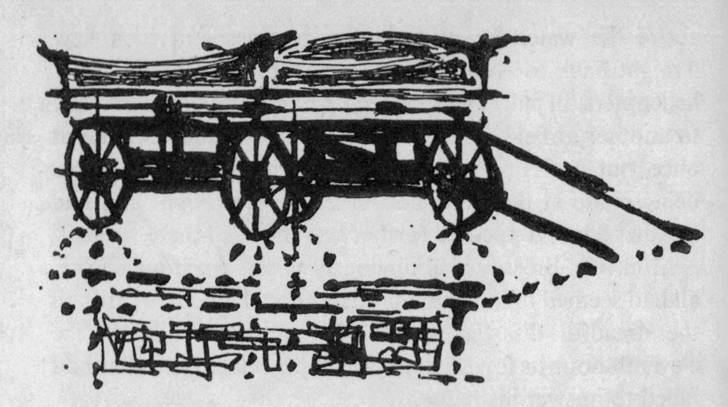

8

The stormy night did no further damage to the devastated area and next day the floods really did begin to go down. The windless sky and the sunshine soon banished all semblance of fear and panic. In a few hours a well-behaved Loire was back in its old bed. First its islands reappeared and then the sandbanks along its edges.

It took the land longer to empty its sodden plough and pasture, woods and orchards. For three days the yellow water poured back through the breaches in the embankment, then, as the level fell still farther, at last it drained into the lazy Authion, whose old meanders reappeared in a single night. The police and the military closed all entry to the ravaged country. Squads from the Public Works Department battled alone to clear the roads and break the dams of sand and mud which here and there formed large lakes.

Meanwhile at Château-Gontier, Monsieur Brossay quickly arranged for his pupils to be sent home. Gradually he saw his beloved flock grow fewer and fewer, until at last, when he had sent his wife and daughter to Nantes, all who were left were the Juillets, the Trévidics and Vignoles, who wanted nothing better than to share the excitement of the return to Château-Milon.

This took place six days later, when the authorities at last granted permission. All the roads between the villages along the embankment and the country behind had been cleared. They found the three vehicles undamaged on the slope of the Arcy woods, but only the blue van could be made to start and then it needed Monsieur Juillet's mighty arm to swing the starting-handle. The task force for Château-Milon soon reached La Bohalle, where they picked up their baggage which had been left there by the coach.

From then on Monsieur Brossay himself took the wheel. He spoke not a word on that short journey back to his property. For six days he had been tormented by anxiety, uncertainty and remorse. There was no news of Monsieur Sala. All inquiries had been lost in the somewhat chaotic organization of the rescue services. At the headmaster's direct request the police had made a swift reconnaissance of the school. They had neither seen nor heard a thing and, as their patrols had more important work to do, they had not stayed long. In any case it would be all too easy to substitute Monsieur Sala's name for one on the long column marked 'unidentified' in the tragically heavy casualty list. Thus Monsieur Brossay expected the worst and, as he drove along, he gloomily composed the little master's obituary notice.

On either side of the narrow lane they could see that the meadows were covered by a three-foot layer of wet sand and clay. Here and there in farm or hamlet life was shyly appearing once more. Here a solitary figure moved, there sheets hung drying from a window sill, here was a puff of smoke as a kitchen fire was lit again, and there a sudden cock-crow rang out across the desert the floods had left behind them.

They neared their objective.

The first thing Vignoles saw in the distance was Mérovée's Tower jutting above the horizon. Like the pile of a jetty, its walls were striped by the successive levels of the water. As they came closer they could see the shattered roofs of Le Plessis and La Vallière, while the roof of the main building itself had been so stripped of its tiles that no more than the bare bones of beam and lath were left. The outer walls seemed to have stood firm, but most of the doors and windows had been washed away by the ebb and flow of the waters. The chapel stood practically undamaged, its grey granite hardly marked.

Monsieur Brossay's face was tense and pale as he parked the van at the top of the drive. Sand and mud blocked the gateway. Caught in the elegant convolutions of the wrought-iron grille, a mass of branches and rubbish hung like a portcullis ten feet above them. They had to climb the bank knee-deep in mud and then scramble on to the mound, on which the mill stood, through the mess and rubbish which covered it.

Then they saw the courtyard. Mud and wreckage was piled to a good three feet round the trunks of the plane trees. When the waters had finally flowed away they had cut a path, littered with boulders, right through this silt and round behind the headmaster's house. It was along this that the little group now began to walk in deathly silence, yard by yard, as though the slightest sound would bring the buildings tumbling about their ears.

Monsieur Brossay went first. As he looked over his shoulder up at Mérovée's Tower his eyes stared, his jaw dropped, the blood fled from his face and he stood rooted to the ground. Someone was leaning out of the skylight calmly watching the newcomers – a scarecrow figure in black, a shapeless black hat topping its head and an untidy thicket of beard ruffing its cheeks.

'S . . . S . . . Sala!' stammered Monsieur Brossay, recognition coming with the flash of the familiar spectacles.

'Monsieur Sala!' sighed Vignoles, laughter struggling with an overwhelming relief.

'The little man himself!' shouted Monsieur Juillet, and the Trévidic brothers gaped in amazement.

Monsieur Sala's voice came ringing down, with a self-assurance unaffected by the distance.

'Good morning, headmaster! Welcome back to Château-Milon!'

Surprise, disbelief, delight and then annoyance chased themselves across the now crimson face of Monsieur Brossay. Annoyance, annoyance tempered by amusement, finally held the field.

'What the devil are you doing up there?' he thundered. 'Come down at once!'

Monsieur Sala raised his arms and let them flop uselessly at his side.

'I can't,' he answered desolately. 'I know it's silly, but the door's locked.'

'Well, break it down, then. Use a little sense!'

His answer made them all feel sorry.

'I didn't dare,' called Monsieur Sala, pointing round. 'The school's suffered enough damage as it is.'

'Hurry down, and mind you don't break your neck. We'll open the door for you.'

Job Trévidic hurried away to find, on its accustomed nail, the key to the massive door of Mérovée's Tower.

A few minutes later they were able to free Monsieur Sala. As he staggered out on his stumpy legs, his wretched appearance – floppy hat, muddy coat, Sunday suit ripped and tied together with bits of string – all these made them sorry for him and at one and the same time want to laugh.

'Really, you are an odd chap!' Monsieur Brossay gave him a friendly pat on the shoulder. 'Here we were, worried to death about you for the last week.'

A radiant Vignoles grinned at the slight figure who had shown such great-heartedness in the crisis through which they had passed. To find him safe and sound drove the last dark clouds away.

'And what on earth happened to you?' Monsieur Brossay exclaimed.

'The stupidest accident that could happen and the most hair-raising in that sort of situation for somebody like me. But you have to be as shortsighted as I am to grasp just how frightening and idiotic it all was... You see, ten minutes before I was due to be taken off that wonderful evening I lost my glasses... There it is in a nutshell.'

'It's ridiculous,' said Monsieur Brossay.

'I know it is!' sighed Monsieur Sala. 'But placed as we had been for those last twenty-four hours the slightest thing could make all the difference... The Alouette had just taken off Vignoles and I had only ten minutes to wait. I felt a little weak at the knees from excitement, so I got down from the skylight, backwards. But I slipped, caught my heel on a cogwheel and fell flat on my back, cracking my head on the edge of the trap-door. I must have knocked myself out for about ten seconds and when I came to – no glasses. I felt all round – nothing. The wretched things had fallen straight through the trap-door and were lying on the floor below under three feet of water. That really was my worst moment. Being so shortsighted, I realized I'd be quite useless in the delicate rescue operations. How on earth was I going to catch the ladder and the safety-line, buckle on the harness and launch myself into space when everything round me was a misty blur? And the light was fading fast. After I'd thought it over, I decided the wisest thing was to pretend I was dead. So I crouched down among the machinery and let the Alouette circle the mill and go away without me. Do you think I did wrong? After all, it was getting dark and if I'd made any distress signals it would only have meant increasing the risks that were being run just to rescue me. I had a roof over my head, so I wasn't all that badly off, and with five lots of bedding and twenty tins of sardines I could hold out for several days. All the same, I did spend a pretty wretched first night!'

'What about your glasses?' Vignoles asked, his voice slightly tinged with suspicion.

'I had to wait for the floods to go down before I could recover them,' Monsieur Sala laughed nervously. 'I followed the water rung by rung down the ladder until on the second day there was only six inches in the flour store-room. I spent a good three hours going over every square foot of floor and at last I found them. The lenses were intact, but the left side was broken. That's why I've got this piece of string dangling from my ear.'

'Did you have any visitors?' asked Monsieur Juillet. 'As we came along the drive I saw footprints in the mud.'

'Yes, first there were the police. I lay low. I was afraid they'd arrest me as a looter. Then yesterday morning I spotted a couple of real looters prowling round the gate.'

'What did you do?' Vignoles asked.

'I shied my empty sardine tins at them through the sky-light,' Monsieur Sala answered calmly. 'I couldn't have done better if I'd fired a shot-gun at them. I've never seen anyone move so fast in my life!'

There was a roar of laughter.

'So you stayed to the bitter end to guard Château-Milon.' Monsieur Brossay was delighted. 'This certainly will make a splash in our report at the end of the school year. I can just see it.'

'But will there be an end of the school year?' Vignoles murmured dubiously.

Monsieur Brossay's face was furrowed as he stared at the buildings.

'It all depends on what we find when we go inside.'

The first thing to do was to survey the damage and to estimate, quite cold-bloodedly, whether it would take three months or three years to put the school on its feet once more.

While Job and Yvon Trévidic took care of Monsieur Sala and fitted up rough and ready living-quarters on the first floor of Le Plessis, Monsieur Brossay and the others had a quick look round the buildings. From outside the damage seemed slight; the walls were sound and the roofs could easily be mended, but within a heart-breaking sight met their eyes. What the floods had not smashed they had reduced to a sodden, mildewed mess.

At first sight Vignoles would have thought it would take three years, always provided, that is, that the necessary money could be raised at once. Oddly enough, Monsieur Brossay was of a different opinion. Perhaps to feel his property beneath his feet and to walk round it was enough to release his boundless energy.

'Château-Milon will reopen for the summer term,' he announced firmly. 'I'll write today to the parents and tell them so. Money? I'll get it if I have to go on bended knees to every Local Authority, Government Department and rich man in the neighbourhood! We sleep here tonight and we stay on the premises from now on. I'm not going to see valuable time going to waste. Madame Juillet and her daughter are needed as soon as possible to do the cooking and save us needless chores. In a couple of days I shall have the first lot of builders on the roofs, doors and windows...'

He paused for breath and swung a baleful glare upon the countryside bathed by the soft December sun.

'What I need to start with,' he bellowed, 'is a fortnight's fine weather!'

His anger must have impressed the immortals, for he had it, and money and workmen and ready cooperation all round.

On the evening of that memorable day, as Job Trévidic was unpacking the sleeping-bags and his brother Yvon laying a scanty table, the cheerful peal of Cunégonde rang through the darkness to call them from their toil to the evening meal. A weary Monsieur Brossay was last into the candlelit hall of Le Plessis. The others were all there, among them Monsieur Sala in a fresh change of clothes and without his beard. The headmaster passed no remarks and asked no questions and no one ever knew who had rung the bell, but from that moment none doubted the rebirth of Château-Milon.

In the course of the next fortnight the masters returned one by one, the first being Father Fabien and the bursar. Neither of them minded the rough living of those early days. When Monsieur Corzon was not bustling round Angers, Rennes or Paris, raising money to swell the reconstruction fund, he seemed to be everywhere in the grounds, chasing slackers, checking the workmen's time sheets, whether they liked it or not, and sieving the rubbish taken from the houses like any miser.

It was piled in one enormous heap in the courtyard, but before he allowed it to be burned he had to sort it through for the last time. For two days the smoke from this bonfire stank the place out. Every so often Monsieur Sala would keep it going with armfuls of sodden paper, and the two thousand five hundred pages of his thesis 'Modern Survivals of Kantian Thought' fed the flames in bundles of one hundred. To them was added a dog-eared copy of *The Critique of Pure Reason*. He protracted this *auto-da-fé* with obvious enjoyment.

'I hope you remember enough to refresh my memory on one or two points,' Vignoles laughed. 'Monsieur Brossay's made me promise to put in four hours a day studying, but it doesn't look to me as though this term'll give me brain fever... Between you and me I think what we're doing at Château-Milon's just as good as preparing for my certificate.'

'I'll keep an eye on you,' Monsieur Sala promised seriously. 'Don't worry, Monsieur Brossay told me the other day that he doesn't allow the use of the dunce's cap even in the bottom forms at Château-Milon – he says it's a barbarous custom which gives its victims a dangerous inferiority complex...'

A few days after Christmas, Monsieur Boris turned up. Work on the school was going ahead at fever pitch and perhaps it was this that persuaded him to turn down the offer of an excellent post in a school at Le Mans. At all events, although he came as a visitor he stayed for good.

By the end of February one wing of the school had been made more than habitable and Madame Brossay and her daughter soon moved in. It was the once unsociable Vignoles who undertook to lead the girl on a conducted tour of the estate and to show her the work in progress.

'These last two weeks have made all the difference,' he told her on their way across the courtyard. 'Now we can say for certain that Château-Milon will reopen after Easter. Of course, there's still plenty to do, but our fifty boys will have the same peace and comfort as before... By the way, I know your father's very concerned about it, and he won't say a word to anyone, but just how well is he making up the numbers?'

'You mustn't tell a soul what I'm going to tell you,' Edith made him promise. 'So far we've only been able to get

thirty of our old pupils back. That would just be enough to keep the school on its feet, but we can't count on all of them. The parents of the others still hum and haw and produce all sorts of reasons which can't hide the truth – they're scared. Father showers them with enthusiastic reports and it's as if the future of the school depended on the people who haven't been able to make up their minds.'

'I'm not worried; they'll all turn up,' Vignoles assured her imperturbably. 'A fortnight ago when it looked as if Muret, Lalande and Montaigu would rat, I sent each one of them an eight-page letter which made them change their parents' minds.'

Their stroll had taken the pair close to La Vallière. In the senior house, its front as clean and freshly painted as it had been before the floods, they were finishing decorating the prep-room and the hall.

Vignoles walked Edith round the building to show her the dormitory balcony.

'That's the way our little group escaped. When I came back in December the ladder was still there. When the water fell it washed one end away from the window in the mill, but the other was still firmly lashed to the balustrade.'

The girl appreciated the way he made light of the dangers of their escape. As she listened, she looked up at the wall, the windows, the skylight in the mill, the gap between the buildings – and the gutter. She remembered the famous sonnet.

'Looking for something, Edith?' Vignoles asked, his eyes twinkling wickedly in the sunlight.

They exchanged conspiratorial grins.

'You *have* changed,' said Edith.

'I'm not the only one. What we've been through has made a difference to all of us.'

'You've been here six years,' the girl went on, 'and I can remember times when we didn't say a word to one another for months on end. And yet you were one of the family; Father told you that often enough.'

'I know,' Vignoles answered, 'but I had to go through all this to realize what he meant.'

They walked off hand in hand to see how the kitchen garden was doing.

'I'll end up by cutting my best friend out,' thought Vignoles when they came back from their stroll. He appreciated the irony of the situation.

Easter fell late that year, so the summer term was to begin at the end of April, on a Tuesday. The spring was forward and its concealing greenery hid the drifts of sand and gravel, the legacy of the floods.

The weather was glorious. The skies of Anjou had regained their legendary softness of cloud-flecked blue. The horizon seemed to expand to the warmth, which had even brought into bloom one or two of the roses against the chapel wall.

Château-Milon was astir at daybreak to prepare for the great day. Monsieur Brossay seemed happy. The new school roll carried the names of the fifty pupils it had lost in the hurried breaking up four months before. To be sure, there were question marks beside several names which had only been listed as possibles, and these five stood for the element of uncertainty in the hours ahead. Monsieur Corzon, however, had high hopes of being able to use his rubber on all those question marks before the day was out.

Monsieur Brossay took the wheel of the 203 to run a taxi service from Angers station, while Monsieur Juillet was to use the Deux Chevaux for those who came by way of Saumur. All the masters were on their toes, dressed in their Sunday best, to form a friendly committee of welcome, prominent among which were Father Fabien's big white beard and Monsieur Sala's gleaming spectacles.

Vignoles watched it all from a grandstand seat, the window of his old room. It was his first real holiday for months and he took good care to parade his idleness shamelessly. From on high he could take in at a glance the domain over which he judged he had some special rights and at the same time make sure that a girl in a light summer frock was reading on the terrace in front of the headmaster's house. The way things were going, Edith felt sure she would soon have to choose between two streams of sonnets which would be showering upon her.

Soon after nine Monsieur Brossay brought his first load

back from Angers – three juniors. Chomel was among them, so that Monsieur Corzon could at once rub out one question mark. It was a good start to the day.

Monsieur Sala took charge of the boys with easy authority and saw them safely installed in Le Plessis, where their old places in prep-room and dormitory were waiting for them.

He took Chomel to one side.

'Are you proposing to go on ragging me this term?' he asked jocularly. 'If it's something you can't help, if it's vital to your physical well-being, you've only to tell me now and we'll come to some arrangement...'

'Oh no, sir! Never, sir!' A reformed character looked him straight in the eye. 'I'll do more, sir. I'll look after the dormitory and the prep-room for you, sir, and if anyone tries anything I'll do him for you!'

Half an hour later Monsieur Juillet brought back from Saumur three seniors and a junior, the two Muret brothers, Lalande, and the bellman, Jeantet. The latter at once leaped to Cunégonde's rope and treated them to an impromptu peal.

The rhythm of successive arrivals was maintained all the morning, so that Madame Juillet had thirty places to lay for lunch. Gradually the rooms in La Vallière were claimed by their owners, but not as fast as Vignoles would have liked. He was still waiting for his fellow prisoners in Mérovée's Tower – Picard, Charpenne and Boisson de Chazelles.

'Who? The Vicomte?' Monsieur Brossay exclaimed on his way back to the station after lunch. 'I wouldn't put my money on him!'

It was hard to guess whether bitterness lurked beneath his offhand manner. In any case, as the day wore on, Château-Milon was regaining the gaiety, the confusion and the bustle traditional to the first day of term. Each boy was free to do as he pleased on that one day, free to re-explore a school which showed few traces of the damage it had suffered, free to meet old friends once more, free to resume the familiar routine, the pleasant blend of discipline and enjoyment.

The football fans hurriedly laced their boots on and, led by Muret and Lalande, raced off to try out the pitch beside the Authion, where the goalposts gleamed in the fresh coat of paint Monsieur Boris had put on them. The clodhoppers of Cunault had taken advantage of the cancelled match of last December to go two points above them in the league table. It was an insult!

Monsieur Juillet and the Trévidic brothers had put the better of the two tennis courts to rights and it was soon surrounded by a mass of players. Traditionally, practical jokes played their part in the excitement of the beginning of term. Nor were they missing now.

Charpenne and Picard were expected on the four o'clock coach from Beaufort. They made it put them down a hundred yards from the drive and then slunk stealthily round the back with their suitcases and slipped in through the garden gate. Vignoles was stretched on the window-sill, sunning himself like a lizard, and he nearly tumbled into the courtyard below when he heard a raucous volley of croaks, laughter and whistles coming from Mérovée's Tower. He looked up and his gaze swung round to see the pair sitting side by side in the skylight, their legs dangling over a forty-foot drop.

A number of pupils, among them the Dubourg brothers, Montaigu, Jozas and Sardine, arrived in all the pomp of their parents' cars. Mothers and fathers drifted across the courtyard, eyeing the battered plane trees and staring incredulously at the sombre streak the highest level of the flood had left on the wall of the old mill. Then they strolled over to the terrace in front of the headmaster's house where Madame Brossay presided over the tea-table.

At five o'clock, when these visitors had departed, Monsieur Brossay and Monsieur Corzon checked the school roll. They looked up at one another and beamed. No one would have believed it four months before, and yet there it was in black and white – there was not one single absentee, unless of course they counted that eccentric nobleman, Boisson de Chazelles, and he had never really been one of the family at Château-Milon.

The pair strolled over to the two houses to make sure all was in order and to enjoy their triumph at the pleasantest part of the day. As they came out of La Vallière, Monsieur Brossay walked by himself to the gate. He was about to close the freshly gilded mass of wrought-ironwork when a taxi drew up in the drive.

Out popped Hubert Boisson de Chazelles like a jack-in-the-box, with his beaky nose, brilliantined hair, light tweed suit and a pair of pigskin suitcases.

'Oh, yes! Here I am!' he said, gravely shaking the headmaster by the hand. 'I've made a solemn promise: renounced the pomps and vanities of the wicked world... My father wanted to send a couple of policemen to see I got here, but something more forceful dragged me back to Château-Milon... Were you expecting me?'

'Yes and no,' Monsieur Brossay answered, hiding his smile. 'At all events there's a bed for you in Vignoles's room and the menu tonight is particularly well chosen... So stay, and if, in future, you feel a change of scene would do you good, just ask me for the front-door key. It will at least save me from catching my death of cold hanging around the back gate!'

'You don't seem exactly delighted to see me back again,' Hubert remarked rather frigidly.

'I'm only sorry you didn't find your way here three years ago,' Monsieur Brossay replied.

'Three months will be quite enough for me to catch up with all that.' The Vicomte's voice was deliberately cold, perhaps to hide a twinge of regret.

Vignoles from his window saw them coming and at once tipped off the others that their noble colleague had arrived. The seniors poured out of their rooms, rushed downstairs and congregated in the hall. With Charpenne to conduct them, they greeted the newcomer with an anthem composed especially for him.

Monsieur Brossay laughed to himself as he walked back to his house. His was the happy privilege of removing the last question mark from the roll and, as he put down his rubber, he stood before the open window wrapped in thought. The flowers were out again in the beds around the courtyard, the trees were in leaf, the boys had come back to Château-Milon, and a spring day was drawing to a close in pink- and gold-tipped clouds. This was the end of the chapter. From the terrors of that December night all had in some degree emerged with characters enhanced.

At that very minute others like him were gazing at the golden sky which seemed to reassure them that spring was really there. The peril which they had surmounted together had changed them all. It had revealed unexpected strength of character, it had dissolved foolish enmities, it had strengthened the ties of friendship, it had cured the selfish and stirred the sluggards.

In a matter of hours Vignoles had learned to love a school where he had so long rejected the family life that had been offered him. The butterfly Charpenne had realized that real feeling is expressed not in plagiarized sonnets, but in the anxiety felt for someone dear to you. The appalling Chomel had in one night of peril cast off his old stupid and mischief-making self. That rolling stone Hubert Boisson de Chazelles had at last realized that team spirit counted for more than rank or wealth and that one unselfish action did more to inspire true comradeship than weeks of showing off. In short, every one of the boys, from tiny Kiki Dubourg to gigantic Picard, had come in his own way through the ordeal. Not one had failed. Through them and for them their school had survived the floods and recovered its physical and spiritual being.

And this was just as true of the amazing Monsieur Sala. That night, as he crossed from La Vallière to Mérovée's Tower on two shaky ladders, he had shed his shyness and made sure that, despite his disastrous beginning, he would find in Château-Milon the haven of sympathetic security best suited to his unpretentious, scholarly way of life.

About the Author

Paul Berna was born at Hyeres in 1913. He was the youngest son of a large, noisy, and quarrelsome family where everybody had a good deal of fun. He spent the whole of his childhood in the South of France, and though circumstances have forced him to spend a lot of time elsewhere he had always been very attached to this part of the country.

He went to school in Toulon and later at Aix, where he did very well, passing his pre-university exam with credit. His great interest in books and literature of every kind went hand in hand with an enthusiasm for football and swimming. After leaving school he did a two year apprenticeship at a Paris bank. This was followed by a number of jobs, none of which really appealed to him. After the Second World War he was offered an administrative job in the Post Office.

In spite of his professional occupations he has always been interested in young people and their books. Indeed all his works show that he has a remarkable insight into the mind of the modern child.

A Hundred Million Francs and *The Secret of the Missing Boat* are also available in Puffins.

In 1960 he married Saint-Marcoux who is well known for her novels for older girls.